A ROCK AND A HARD PLACE

NIKKY KAYE

 Created with Vellum

CONTENTS

Coming Attractions   v

A ROCK

1. Evie   3
2. Evie   11
3. Dominic   21
4. Evie   31
5. Jake   40
6. Evie   46
7. Dominic   58
8. Jake   70
9. Evie   81
10. Evie   90
11. Evie   99
12. Dominic   105
13. Evie   112

A HARD PLACE

1. Annie   125
2. Jake   134
3. Annie   142
4. Jake   152
5. Annie   160
6. Annie   168
7. Jake   179
8. Annie   187
9. Annie   197

10. Jake   208
11. Jake   218
12. Annie   225
13. Annie   234
14. Jake   242
15. Annie   248
16. Annie   256
17. Jake   261
18. Jake   266
19. Annie   271

Also by Nikky Kaye   279
Acknowledgments   281
About the Author   283

COMING ATTRACTIONS

These books are a crazy ride! The first novella in this duet was published in July 2017 under the title *Bought By the Billionaire Brothers*. The much-requested follow-up, *Saved by the Single Dad SEAL*, was published in October 2017.

Readers loved the stories, but they were only available for a very short time in 2017, and also briefly on the market again in Summer 2018 (rebranded as *The Fox* and *The Hound*).

Now they have been extensively edited, and I'm thrilled to reintroduce them together as **A ROCK AND A HARD PLACE**. They were a pure joy to write, rediscover, then write again. I hope you enjoy them as much as I do.

Head's up: There are MFM (threesome, ménage, whatever you want to call it) encounters in the first part. If that's not your thing, then just flip fast. There is no cheating, and lots of happy endings to look forwards to, but it is not a traditional *ménage à trois* trope.

I'll confess—I've never written anything this smutty

before. Sexy, yes. But some of this is downright… dirty. *Gulp!*

Remember—read safely. One-handed reading should only be done in the comfort and security of your own home (wink wink).

For sneak peeks at new books, contests, and other fun, free stuff, join my mailing list by going to http://subscribepage.com/nikkykaye or http://nikkykaye.com to sign up.

xoxo, Nikky

August 2019

A ROCK

EVIE

"*T*his is, without a doubt, the craziest idea I've ever had." I shook my head, unable to look away from the insanity on the screen of my laptop.

"And yet you're actually doing it. That's even more whackadoo."

My next-door neighbor and new best friend Annie squinted as she peered into an empty wine bottle. Her idea of getting together for a Friday night drink meant I drank one glass and she polished off the rest.

If only I was tipsy. That would explain what I was about to do. *Oh dear god.*

"I can't do this." My heart raced in my chest.

"Sure, you can. What have you got so far?" Annie stood up from the couch, swayed a little, then stumbled the few steps through my tiny apartment to where I sat at my kitchen table.

"Kitchen" was a generous label, actually, since I had a bar fridge, a microwave, and a hot plate—plus a sink. It was like living in a small RV that didn't go anywhere. The little secondhand café table where Annie hovered over me was my dining room slash home office, and it was about as rickety as my judgment right now.

She read out loud, *"College graduate ready to sell V-card. Not ugly, just shy and a little fluffy."* Her bark of laughter ended up in a hiccup, and she grabbed the back of the chair I sat on.

My face heated as she leaned over my shoulder in a fit of drunken giggles.

"Oh my god, that's awesome," she wheezed.

I had *not* had enough wine for this. I shoved her away with my shoulder. "Yeah, well, it's not like I have a lot of experience with this."

"That's the point, Evie." Sobering briefly, she rested her hip against the table and crossed her arms. "Are you sure about this, kiddo? It's kind of… important."

Was it? I told myself that losing your V-card was only a big deal in popular culture, and that its significance was merely a social construct borne of hundreds of years of patriarchy and misogyny.

It didn't really mean anything. There was probably a first time a person picked their nose, too, but that wasn't ritualized in romance novels. Why, then, was my heart racing like I'd been mainlining coffee instead of a glass of cabernet?

"The ends justify the means, Annie," I said firmly. "Besides, it's a hymen, not a retirement fund. Most people don't save it for a rainy day. I gotta lose it some-time. It might as well be for a good cause."

"You know I'd help you if I could." She made her way back to the couch and sat down with a sad sigh.

I turned to look at her, resting my chin on my arms on the back of the ugly wooden chair, my dirty blonde hair curling where it hit my shrugged shoulders.

"Waitresses don't make that much money, Annie. I know. But thanks."

Annie was funny, sweet, and as broke as I was. She had ten years of life experience on me, but at least she didn't have close to a hundred thousand dollars in debt hanging over her head. The interest alone was killing me.

I'd spent enough of the last year plagued by fear and anxiety, nightmares and cold sweats.

My fancy degree was utterly useless in today's economy. I'd gone with my heart, not my head, when I'd chosen to major in comparative literature. My grades weren't good enough to get me scholarships, but my parents and I were thrilled when I still got into my first choice college.

I hadn't known that my parents had taken out a second mortgage to leverage my student loans until they died soon after I graduated. Ironically, it was the house that killed them, with carbon monoxide.

It all, well… it sucked.

The threat of yet more tears pricked at my nose, and I swiveled back to stare at my computer screen. I kept thinking I was all cried out, until…

"What about a picture?" Annie asked. "You need a photo of the goods, Evie."

"*What?* You want me to take a selfie of my *hooha*?"

"I think a bra and panties shot will do it. And you might not want to call it your hooha in the ad, Miss Priss." She tilted her head. "Actually, go ahead. You might get more bids from creepy old men looking to play Daddy."

She was joking, but I squirmed in my chair.

I didn't want to admit it, but the idea of letting

someone take care of me made my skimpy sleep shorts a little damp. It shouldn't have made me hot, but neither should have all the smutty fan fiction I'd been reading as of late.

Maybe it was because I missed having human contact. Annie was great, but she wasn't the touchy feely type. I'd moved to a cheaper city, hoping to save more money, but that meant leaving everyone I knew behind.

At the time, I'd told myself that I was starting over, but I realized too late that it was an escape, and a bad one at that.

Now I had to hug myself, touch myself when I felt... ornery, and it just left me feeling lonelier.

I missed having people, having a family. Being an orphan—the only child of only children—was sad, to say the least.

Being a broke orphan was... desperate.

"I should add 'looking for Daddy Warbucks' while I'm at it," I muttered. "How pathetic."

Self-pity wasn't going to get me anywhere, but sometimes it was a tempting rabbit hole to fall into. I stared into space, lost in a dreamland somewhere between sexual fantasy and sad memories.

It wasn't until I heard the door slam that I realized Annie had gone next door to her apartment and just returned. I blinked at her.

"Reinforcements." She brandished another bottle of wine and an evil grin.

Oh dear god.

~

I woke up Saturday morning with my head spinning.

Thank god I shoved my narrow bed against the wall, to use as a second couch. If I looked over the side right now, there was a better than even chance I'd fall off. My mind lurched along with my stomach as I tried to remember where Annie and I had left off last night.

Shit.

My heart whumped in my chest as I saw that my laptop wasn't on the table anymore. It was on the couch, as closed and secretive as my hooha.

About the same time, my brain registered that I wasn't wearing my sleep shorts and tank top anymore. Somehow, I had managed to pass out in the most uncomfortable, sexiest bra and panty set I *didn't* own.

A vague memory came back to me of at least one more glass of wine and Annie bringing over a selection of lingerie, claiming we were "around the same size." Not true, judging by the way my ample curves were spilling out of the white lacy push-up bra. But why—oh! Pictures!

Shit, pictures!

I jumped off the bed. Adjusted and wriggled a little. I sat on the couch and opened the computer on my lap. Wriggled more. *How the hell did Annie wear thongs like this?* I wondered.

As the laptop took its time waking up, and I found myself praying to the god of small mercies that we hadn't actually—

Your profile has been completed! Please check your inbox for the confirmation email.

"Fuck!"

My chest hurt as I tried to hold my panic in. I bit my lip—hard—as the computer's battery warmed my bare thighs.

What was I expecting? The gods had never been kind to me—why would they start now?

Chest heaving and stomach dropping, I clicked through to my inbox, where the confirmation taunted me. Then I went back to the web profile, horrified to discover messages in that inbox as the page refreshed.

It was still loading.

Fuck fuck fuckity fuck.

154 messages. I gaped at the screen. Were virgins so thin on the ground these days that a brief bio and a boob shot constituted the Second Coming? *Apparently so*, I thought, until I checked on my "brief bio and boob shot."

My lips made the shape of the words and my throat formed the sounds, but my brain still had trouble processing the editorial changes that Annie had made.

"Prestigious college… saved my cherry for you… innocent and eager to please… just want to be *loved*?"

Annie!

After reading that, I almost didn't want to see what pictures she'd posted of me. I don't remember being that far into our "photo shoot" before I crashed. That second bottle of wine had been a bad, bad idea.

Sure enough, the thumbnail I clicked on revealed me sprawled seductively on the tiny couch, my D-cups falling out of Annie's B-cup bra and my arms up near my head, like I was combing my hair with my fingers. At least my thick thighs were closed, and all you could see of the ivory thong was the lacy string digging into the fleshy padding at my hip.

I looked sexy; I couldn't deny it.

Looking at the picture even made me *feel* sexy for once. Being curvy in a culture that valued lollipop-head girls had certainly contributed to my virginal status.

Sexy. Me.

They were two words I'd never put together, until now. I was tempted to prance around like a plus-size supermodel, except for the fact that Annie's thong was so damn uncomfortable.

However I felt about doing this, it had been done. The Internet allowed for lots of regret but little recourse, especially with something like this.

Morbid curiosity compelled me to read the emails. It was like the urge to slow down assess the damage when you drive past a car crash. Some messages were filthy, while others were just raunchy. Most were surprisingly short and to the point.

The vast majority of them had dick pics attached. *Seriously? Who does that?* Reflexively, I glanced around, like someone was watching me. I felt weird just looking at someone's junk on my computer screen.

This is why you're still a virgin, Evie.

I hadn't realized private parts could be so... public. They were all so different, at least until they started to blur together. I took a deep breath. Then another. A woozy feeling came over me, which I hoped was just a hangover.

If seeing naked boy parts nauseated me, then the whole "selling my virginity" thing was *not* going to go well. I was going to have to get over this. If I had no problems reading steamy books, why did pictures make me nervous?

After a deep, cleansing breath, I opened up Tumblr in another tab. Within a minute I found more nudity than I'd ever seen in one place—mostly genuinely sexy, not icky pornographic. Satisfied that I was adequately desensitized, I went back to the emails still coming in.

I skimmed through some offers, my eyes widening as I realized how valuable my innocence was. Sure, some bids would barely buy me dinner at a nice restaurant, but others would pay my rent, even buy me a car—and not a shitty used one.

There was one email, however, that made me sit back, my fingers sweating on the track pad.

It was polite but suggestive, articulate but not stuffy. In fact, it was a shockingly formal proposition, almost like a job offer. With a lot of zeros. And no dick pics.

It couldn't hurt to email back, right?

Slowly, I pecked out a response, asking some pertinent questions. How did one politely ask, "why the hell are you bidding on a girl's virginity online?" When I was done, I closed my eyes as I clicked on send before parking my laptop on the couch beside me.

Then I went to throw up.

EVIE

$\mathcal{N}$ow *this* was the craziest thing I'd ever done.

No, the stupidest, I thought to myself as I walked through the lobby of the gleaming skyscraper.

I was here to meet with Dominic Stone—Mister Whole-Lotta-Zeros.

We'd emailed back and forth to discuss the terms of my "deflowering." He'd encouraged me to do an Internet search on him, which provided me with a visual of my potential, uh, "gardener"—a smoking hot one.

Dark hair, dark eyes, dark look.

There were pictures of him at charity events, in business magazine profiles, and the odd paparazzi shot of him coming out of the gym. Dominic Stone looked good in gym clothes. And suits. And tuxedos.

There weren't a lot of pictures of him with dates, though. Maybe he was gay? I thought that might have been the case when I saw another ridiculously attractive specimen beside him in a lot of the pictures, but that turned out to be his brother Jacob.

I didn't get it. Neither of these men needed to buy a

virgin online. They were, quite literally, panty-droppers. If their square jaws and bedroom eyes didn't do it for the ladies, then their suggestive grins certainly would.

It did for me, anyhow.

I'd spent a long time looking at the pictures. Even in thumbnail size, Dominic Stone's power and magnetism practically radiated off the screen. Would he be the one? The idea made my body heat up and my nipples tighten. My breath shortened and a curling, pulsing sensation built low in my belly.

Okay, I wished he *had* sent a dick pic.

After a lot of back and forth, I'd agreed to meet him at his office. It was actually his building, I realized as I saw the signs in the lobby.

Dominic and Jacob Stone ran one of the biggest retail conglomerates in the country. It owned a boutique department store, a chain of high-end media stores, a ubiquitous box store, and god only knew what else. The zeros he'd offered in his email were totally legit.

I once promised myself that I'd never work in retail. That could change.

As instructed, I told the man at the security desk that I was there to see Mister Stone.

He didn't even take his eyes off his magazine. "You can go up to the twelfth floor, ma'am. They'll help you there."

"He said he'd come down to meet me." *Ma'am? Really?* I was twenty-two, not twice that!

Mister Stone—Dominic—had insisted we meet first in the lobby, as a kind of show of good faith and safety. Meeting in a public place, he'd written, was a good idea for all parties concerned in this potential transaction. With dozens of people floating in and out of the elevators of the thirty-story building, it couldn't be much more public.

With a sigh, the guard reached for the phone. "Have a seat." He gestured towards a leather bench.

No, thank you. I needed to move.

My nerves were getting the better of me, my hands shaky and cold despite the summer heat. If I stood, my sleeveless red sheath dress wouldn't wrinkle.

When I got up that morning, I had to decide what one wore to an interview as a… what? Mistress? No— that sounded too committed. Hymen vendor? *Ugh.* In the end, I decided to dress as though going to work, which was kind of true.

My heels clicked on the polished stone floor as I walked over to an abstract metal sculpture on display. It stretched nearly twenty feet in the air, shining in the morning sun bending through the floor-to-ceiling windows.

"What do you think?" a man asked from behind me. It was probably the security guard, making sure I didn't touch it.

"It's beautiful." I held up my hands. "I promise, I won't go any closer."

"Hmm." His voice was nearer. "What was the first word that came to mind when you walked in?"

I frowned at the odd question. "It looks delicate." Like it could fall over any minute, like metal pick-up sticks stacked dangerously high.

"There's over a thousand wire coat hangers there."

"Huh." So there was.

"You are Evie, correct?"

Swallowing hard, I turned to the voice. And looked up.

Dominic Stone stood before me, his tall, dark and handsome figure like a shadow in the sunlit lobby.

He was even hotter in person.

Even if his charcoal suit came from a discount store —which it clearly didn't—his attitude would be enough to command my attention. All those fanciful words, like charismatic, magnetic, and imposing, were all very appropriate when describing Dominic Stone.

My three-inch heels barely took me to his shoulders, and I wobbled a little as his gaze ran over me. Just when I was about to turn my ankle, his hand shot out. The feel of his muscular forearm under my fingers had the exact opposite effect of steadying me.

"Thanks." My face burned, but I forced myself to look him in the eye.

They were rich, dark brown, as heady as strong coffee and gave me a similar jolt. When he tilted his head and his lips curved at the edges, I couldn't tell if I amused him or he was just being polite.

A furrow appeared between his dark eyebrows. "You are Evie, right?"

"Yes!" I squeezed his arm, as though I subconsciously expected him to run away.

Instead of shrugging me off, he used his other hand to tug my fingers down his wrist to end in a warm, tingling handshake. Both his hands were around mine, and he didn't let go.

I didn't mind.

"It's a pleasure to meet you," he said smoothly. "Shall we?"

Shall we what? I blinked at him.

"Go up to my office?" He nodded toward the

elevator bank. "Unless you'd feel better staying here? Or we could go get a coffee or something."

I stared at him, the absurdity of this situation dawning on me. And then my big smart mouth got ahead of my brain.

"Coffee? Does my virginity come with an espresso and a muffin?"

His laugh sounded like a sharp bark, echoing off the stone floor. My face probably matched the crimson of my dress as I looked down. With his hands still wrapped around mine, he pulled me closer. I shivered as his warm breath caressed my bare shoulders.

"No, Evie, I'll pay extra for the coffee. But I like it sweet and milky, not dark and bitter."

What was I supposed to say to that? My brain hadn't gotten beyond processing the sensation of his hard fingers brushing over the veins at the inside of my wrist, or his light, crisp scent. In contrast to his dark good looks, he smelled like... the beach.

This time, when I swayed toward him, I couldn't blame my stilettos.

"Your office is fine," I said faintly.

"Excellent."

I let him guide me to the elevators, past the disinterested security guard. We ascended so quickly that my insides felt weightless when we stopped.

He still held my hand in one of his, as though afraid to lose me. Wordlessly, he led me past a small forest of cubicle-dwellers, down a hallway, and into a large corner office. He gestured to a seating area on one side of the room, with a modern-looking brown leather couch and a couple of matching chairs.

"Would you prefer that I leave the door open?"

"That's okay. I'd rather have the privacy, if it's all the same to you."

What did he think I was afraid of? That he'd assault me? Pin me down to his desk and take advantage of me? Wasn't that kind of the whole point of this? *Well, let's get to it, then, and get out your checkbook.* All this went through my head in the few seconds it took him to close the door.

He strode over to his massive wooden desk with purpose, jiggling his mouse to wake up his computer. My knee was bumping up and down nervously as he threw me a smile.

"This will just take a second," he assured me, before tapping something out on the keyboard.

The suspense was killing me.

Click clackety click.

Now both my knees were shaking, and I spread my palms over them to try to keep them still. The narrow skirt of the dress I wore ensured that my seated pose on the brown leather couch remained ladylike, with my legs pressed together and my ankles crossed demurely.

As Dominic Stone walked back over to me our gazes met. I'd always thought the term "eye fucking" was a little over the top—until now. His expression was frankly admiring and would have made me nervous, if it didn't instead make me feel like a million dollars. Which reminded me…

"Um, Mister Stone—"

"Dom." He stood in front of me where I sat on the couch, his belt buckle squarely in my line of sight.

He was a Dom? My hand flew to my mouth to hide my shocked giggle. I may have been a virgin, but I was an avid romance reader. Kinky stuff, sometimes. Was I supposed to call him Master now?

Oh, wait. Dom was short for Dominic. I was officially a clueless idiot.

"About my profile," I began again. "It isn't exactly, totally, one hundred percent accurate."

"You're not a virgin?"

"No, that part is accurate." *One thousand percent.*

His hands went to his hips, drawing my eyes to his crotch again. I looked down at my own lap.

"I mean—I am a virgin." *And about to die of embarrassment.* "But the other stuff... well, I didn't write it. My friend did."

He sat down in the armchair placed at a ninety-degree angle to the couch I was perched on. When I looked up at him, his eyes were narrowed. "You went to a good school? You have a degree?"

"Yes."

"Innocent?" He arched an eyebrow. "Eager to please?" he quoted the ad.

My face flamed. "Sort of."

Silence swelled between us. I crossed my ankles the other way, feeling fidgety.

"Would you like to elaborate, Evie?"

Not really. "It's not like I took some abstinence vow and have been saving myself for marriage. It just never happened."

"Do you like men?" His knees spreading a little in his seat, he leaned forward and rested his elbows on his thighs. With his palms together and his forefingers pointed under his chin, he watched me intently.

"Sure." I swallowed, again feeling his attention like a physical touch on my skin. It occurred to me that, compared to Dominic Stone, I'd met a lot of boys, not men.

"I've dated," I said. "It's just—nobody ever did it for me, turned my crank, you know? But I'm not ashamed of it. I'm not walking around with a giant red V on my shirt." My chin went up.

Reflexively his gaze went to my chest. As if on command, my nipples tightened, pressing against the thin lace of my bra and the linen of my dress. "No, no you're not," he murmured. "Do you think I could—how did you put it—'do it' for you?"

I hesitated.

He leaned closer, his hands leaving his chin to trace circles on my bare knees, just below the hem of my dress. "Evie, answer me."

"Yes, Dom."

He spread his palms over my knees. I inhaled sharply as he splayed his long fingers up my thighs.

"Do you find me attractive?" he asked.

Attractive? He was a damn industrial magnet. But surely he didn't need me to boost his ego. "D-d-does it matter?"

"I think it matters very much. This shouldn't be something to 'get through,' like you said in your email. You already explained your reasons for doing this, regardless of who posted your profile. They're under-standable—honorable, even."

The sympathy in his voice made my nose prickle threateningly. *Damn.* "You don't know me. Maybe I'm just a mercenary whore."

"I don't think so." He shook his head. "I think you're a beautiful, intelligent, kind young woman who has had some shitty luck and you're doing what you need to do. I get that."

"You do?" I successfully blinked away the threat of tears.

"Oh yes, I understand. More than you know," he said mysteriously. His hands slid from my legs, leaving a ghostly trail on my skin.

I shivered, feeling untethered. Curious. "What is it that *you* need to do?"

He waved his hand. "We'll get to that. I'll tell you what I *want* to do, Evie. I want to spoil you. I want to show you how amazing your body can feel, and watch your face and hear the noises you make when you come around me."

Holy shit. He didn't need his hands to hold me still and in place, because his words had accomplished that just fine.

"I know what you've been through. I have the reports. But I'm not a rapist, any more than you're a whore."

I gasped.

His husky voice spilled over my skin like a hot shower. "I want you to *fucking love it*, Evie. Crave it. I want you to *beg me* to taste your tender pussy, and make you come so many times on my face that your succulent little clit can't take any more. But only after all that—a *lot* of all that—do I want to sink my dick into you and fill you with my cum."

Breathing... difficult... heart... pounding. *Wait, 'reports'?*

"So yes, it matters if you're attracted to me," he continued. "And I believe you are, just the same as I'm hard as a fucking rock just smelling you right now."

My mouth fell open, but I couldn't make a sound as I looked in his dark eyes. Something low in my belly throbbed, a primitive response to his outrageously carnal whispers. The story he told, no matter how brief, took me to a state of physical longing that I'd never experienced.

I wanted to be his.

At that moment, I knew that at some point I would be thoroughly fucked by this man, but he was wrong—I *already* craved it. I licked my lips, my mouth as dry as my panties were wet.

"Are you eager to please me, Evie?"

"Yes, Dom," I answered automatically. Breathlessly.

The corners of his mouth turned up. He patted my knee. "Good girl. Now, we want to renegotiate the terms."

"*We?*"

It wasn't until he inclined his head toward the door that I realized we weren't alone. His brother Jacob leaned against the closed door, his arms crossed over his chest and his erection visible through his dress slacks.

Oh god. What was I getting myself into, here?

DOMINIC

*E*vie's lovely face paled then flushed pink as she saw my brother by the door.

"How far did you get, Dom?" Jacob asked me.

"Not that far." I hadn't broached this in our email conversations, thinking that it was more of an "in person" topic.

Evie looked between the two of us. I could almost see the wheels spinning in her brain, and her body language folding in herself. *Damn it!*

"You should have waited, Jake," I growled.

Evie was special; I could see that already. And impatient, impetuous Jake was going to blow it—for all of us. It didn't help that his perpetual hard-on was front and center. But that wasn't anything new.

For Jake, every day was casual Friday. Even wearing expensive slacks and a custom tailored shirt, he looked like he just rolled out of someone else's bed.—even though I knew he hadn't. He'd fit in well on a college football team, his light brown hair, blue eyes and quarterback physique drawing women like flies.

He was the light to my dark, and we'd fought over our share of women in the past.

Jake ribbed me for taking things too seriously at times, but on the flip side his approach to everything was casual to the point of dismissiveness.

Until now.

"I'm Jacob. Jake, if you like. Hell, *I'd* like it if you called me Jake." He flashed Evie a smile and stepped toward her with his hand outstretched. She shook it, glancing over at me with a wordless question in her eyes.

"Mister Sto—Dom—should I take this to mean that you're, um, rescinding your offer?" The lust and heat that I'd teased out of her only a few minutes before was giving way to anguish in her eyes.

"No, Evie," I assured her. "We just want to amend it. The amount we discussed over email stands—as a one-time payment. However, if you will consider some different terms, the remuneration would be much more significant."

She frowned. "I don't understand."

"This is a family business. It started with our grand-father, who was, well—"

"A mean, old sonofabitch," Jake offered.

"—a determined entrepreneur." I glared at my brother. "To make a long story short... thanks to the complex terms of his will, we need an heir in order to hang on to the company."

"An heir," she echoed. "Like a baby?"

I nodded. "That's where you come in."

"That's where you *come*," Jake joked. *Idiot.*

She looked between us. "And you need a virgin mother for this? Maybe you should be going to church socials instead of trolling online."

Finally! There was the Evie that I'd met over email. I'd been wondering where that sassy, acerbic woman was. The girl sitting in my office was sexy as sin, but I wanted to know how far I could push her.

"I agree it's a bit old-fashioned, but so is Grandad."

"Old-fashioned? It's downright medieval!" She bolted to her feet, wincing as she turned an ankle in her heels. "Don't you, I don't know, date like normal people?"

Jake snorted. "Baby, you're the one selling yourself online."

She inhaled sharply.

"Shut up, Jake." I held my hand out to her. Thankfully, she let me take hers and lead her over to the chairs in front of my desk. Jake commandeered the couch, and I suspected she might be more comfortable with a bit more space.

As Evie sat in the visitor's chair, the hem of her red dress rose up her creamy thighs, making my mouth dry. A vision of her spread out on my desk danced in my brain.

How naughty would she look bent forward, her arms stretched out above her and her dress above her waist?

Or just sitting on the edge, her legs wrapped around my hips and her panties showing?

Begging me to take her, dripping with arousal, whimpering with need.

"Evie," I said softly, holding her chin to look her straight in the eye. "We can get to those… negotiations later. We're getting ahead of ourselves. Right now I'd like to assess our compatibility."

Her eyes widened. "Compat—"

"Fuckability," Jake offered.

"Shut. *Up!*" I snarled at him. With a sigh, I tried to soften my tone and expression as I focused on Evie again. "Let me ask you, did you receive lots of, er, applications?"

She nodded, biting her lower lip. "More than I expected." Her giggle was one of the sexiest sounds I'd ever heard—so far. If I had my way, it was just the beginning. Jake's chuckle grated on my nerves, but I held her attention.

"How many have you met with?"

Her lashes swept over her cheeks as she looked down, and held up one finger.

One man? "Other than me?"

She curled her finger down back into her fist and shook her head lightly.

Ah. Only me. Satisfaction and pride swelled within me at the revelation. She could be all mine—all ours.

"Not to sound too crude—" *Who was I kidding? We were discussing buying her virginity.* "—but were the initial terms we discussed agreeable to you?" I reminded her of the amount we'd arrived at—the one that prompted her into arranging our meeting.

"Yes, but it wasn't just about the money," she confessed before slapping her hand over her mouth.

"No?" I tugged her hand away from her face, my thumb tracing her lips as they parted.

"You were, well, polite." She blushed. "It sounded almost like a job offer."

"It is, sweetheart," Jake called out from the couch. My hand whipped up to silence him.

"And that appealed to you?" I asked. She nodded. "Well, then, maybe we need to do some entry-level testing, to see where you fit with the organization."

She rolled her eyes. "Businessmen," she muttered under her breath.

Then she gasped as I reached under her dress and unerringly found her damp, cotton-clad slit.

"Dom!"

"Yes, Evie?"

Her eyes narrowed into slits. "I'd like you to at least kiss me before you finger me."

Now it was my turn to be shocked. And delighted. "As you wish, Evie."

I hauled her into my arms and captured her mouth hungrily. Thank god she'd said something, as I didn't know how much longer I could wait. Now that I had her warm, pillowy softness in my arms, I might never let go.

The appreciative murmur from my brother barely registered as my tongue swept into Evie's mouth. I couldn't get enough of her her smell, the silky feel of her skin under my hands. I wanted to taste every inch of her.

"Do you like me kissing you, Evie?" I asked, my mouth wandering over her cheekbones to her earlobes.

She shivered as I stuck the tip of my tongue through one of her little gold hoop earrings. "Yes, Dom. More?"

"Your wish is my command," I said.

More like I would command all her wishes from now on, I thought to myself.

My cock was like concrete in my slacks, and out of the corner of my eye I saw Jacob slouch down on the couch and begin to unbutton his pants. As he reached inside, his grunt caught Evie's attention.

"Oh!" But instead of pulling away, her breath sped up and her body stiffened and burned in my arms.

"Does that turn you on?" I asked. "Watching him?"

Her face was red. "A little."

Her fingertips clawed at my chest, idly going to the buttons of my shirt. The beautiful girl wanted to undress me, even if she didn't know it.

How lucky was I—were *we*—to discover this virginal gem?

I didn't believe in fate, since "fate" had fucked me over more than once with women. I believed in contracts and understandings and vested interests. But this girl was making me lose my head already. I hadn't meant to show my hand so early, but Jake pushed the envelope, as usual.

Luckily, we hadn't scared her off—yet.

"More?" she whispered.

I groaned. "How much?" *How far would she let us take this today, here in my office?* "How much experience have you had, little Evie?"

She trailed her fingers down to my waist. "Enough to know that I want to see your cock, Dominic. I want to taste it." Her rosy cheeks belied her bravado, though.

Fuck, this girl was going to be the death of me. But what a way to go!

"I'm not going to fuck you today, Evie."

I sucked in a sharp breath when she reached inside my boxer briefs and pulled out my throbbing, aching dick. Maybe she didn't hear me.

"I wasn't going to let you," she said. "I just want… more."

Jake grunted from the corner, his hand jerking his erection mercilessly. He had no shame, and for once I admired that about him. What would it feel like now to have no compunction, no hesitation about—

"Ahhh!"

Evie had dropped to her knees to take me in her mouth.

"Fuck, baby, *yes*," I hissed. "Such a good girl. Oh god, your mouth—it's so hot. Is your pussy this hot and wet, too?"

She whimpered, her left hand awkwardly trying to dive underneath her dress.

"I got this," Jake drawled. He jumped to his feet, his long, thick cock thrusting up over his belly, bobbing slightly as he strode over to us.

"Use your hands on me, too," I urged her. "Jake will take care of you."

And he did. He knelt behind her, bunching up her dress in his hands and exposing her simple cotton panties. She let out a moan as he explored her damp center.

I was wholly distracted by her hot little hands cradling my balls while she attempted to deep throat me. Her cunt was probably ten kinds of heaven right now, but all I could feel was the soft palate of her mouth rubbing against the sensitive tip of my dick.

"She's drenched, but these panties have got to go," Jake said, and she swallowed around me as he ripped the thin cotton apart.

I was getting too close, too quickly. "*Ungh*, Evie! Baby, do you want me to come down your throat?"

Her hands squeezed my balls gently before traveling back to cup my ass. She pulled me closer, and I inched down her throat a little bit more. When she looked up at me, her eyes were watering and her pretty mouth stretched wide around my cock.

"Her clit is all puffed up, bro!" Jake announced, like

he was prospecting for gold down there. And, for all intents and purposes, he was.

She made a choking sound and jerked as he pressed her button, tweaking and strumming her little bundle of nerves. I had to give it to him—when my lazy-ass brother wanted to multitask, he could. At the moment he had one hand up her skirt and the other wrapped around his erection.

Evie still hadn't answered my question, though. I wasn't such an asshole that I would flood a woman's mouth without permission. Her nostrils flared, and I could tell by her red face that breathing was a little challenging.

So close… But not now.

I spread my thumbs over the delicate arches of her eyebrows, underneath the crease of concentration in her forehead. "Good girl," I crooned. "But you're not ready."

She looked a little dazed as I reluctantly pushed her off my cock.

"Help her up," I ordered Jake.

As soon as she stood up, I spun her around so her ass was at the edge of the desk. "More?" I asked.

She nodded, her body arching as she lay back on the desk with her dress pushed up.

"Look at that pretty pussy, man!"

For once, I had to agree with Jake's enthusiasm. She was fucking gorgeous. We each pushed one of her legs back gently, her knees bending toward her armpits.

She gasped. "*Oh my god*! I'm so… so…"

"I know, baby."

Evie was exposed and on display in a way she'd

probably never experienced before. Her trust in us was awe-inspiring. Either that, or she was just that naïve.

With the two of us holding her open, we took turns circling the entrance to her slick cunt with our fingers, our tongues, our thumbs. All the while, we kept one hand on our own arousal, trying to hold off as long as we could.

Call me twisted, but I'd shared girls with my brother before. Not often simultaneously, however, and never as blatantly and openly as this. But we seemed to agree that there was something different about Evie.

She cried out and bucked, her hands reaching for us. "Is this—? Oh fuck, I'm going to come? Oh *nooooooooooo*!" The viciousness of her orgasm took her by surprise, judging by the shocked sounds coming from her ruby lips.

Jake was lucky enough to be fucking her with his tongue as she exploded, and he greedily drank up her juices. I palmed her tits roughly, needing more. *More.*

"Evie, I'm going to come on you," I warned her. I wouldn't enter her, but I was desperate to see her pretty pink cunt covered in my cream.

Her head rolled from side to side, her chest heaving and her hips twitching as she continued to come from Jake's ministrations.

He stood with a pained grunt. It only took a quick glance at each other, then the glistening, rosy display of femininity before us, and we were on the same page.

"Just relax, Evie. We'll take care of you. We'll always take care of you," I promised. Then we stood before her and let go.

She flinched when we sprayed her, the hot, sticky sensation surely a new experience for her. Her body curled up as she lifted her head to look down. We'd let go of her legs, but her heels remained on the edge of the desk and her knees fell to the side in a flexible display of submission.

After Jake let out his last rough grunt, he stumbled back a little, finding the couch and sprawling on it with his dick hanging out of his pants. He looked dazed.

Drained but invigorated, I impulsively rubbed my seed into her entrance, fascinated by the way her greedy pussy grasped my fingers. She panted softly, her breathing slowing.

With shaking hands, she tried to tug her dress back down. I helped her as she wriggled her hips, then I pulled her up to a sitting position.

Her eyes were shining, her cheeks red. But she looked me straight in the eye, which I didn't expect.

"So, I guess we're compatible?" she said.

EVIE

I never did find my underwear before I left Dominic Stone's office. I managed to recover a little of my composure, though.

What. The. Fuck. Was that?

Granted, I didn't have a lot of sexual experience, but that was one of the craziest, hottest things that had ever happened to me, and it wasn't even the main act! Talk about jumping in at the deep end.

It was so... raw.

I was still a little dazed when Jake helped me into a cab, dropping a kiss on my cheek and promising to call me later. Dom stood on the sidewalk, rubbing his chin thoughtfully like a villain from a cartoon. His body language was stiff when he said goodbye, but I felt his stickiness between my thighs all the way home.

Annie wasn't home, thankfully. I didn't think I could deal with her inquisition at that moment. My dress was wrinkled and my face hot, but hopefully nobody else could tell that I'd let myself be covered with the semen of two hot billionaire brothers, in their workplace. The more I thought about it, the more shocked I was.

Oh my god. This is insane.

I stood under the shower, feeling my insides pulse at the memories. The water wasn't washing away the arousal once again building at my core. I drew my finger through it lazily, biting my lip when I touched my over-sensitive clit. The clit that Dom and Jake had licked, sucked, toyed with and owned.

And… a baby? He wanted me to be his baby mama? We never got to that part of the negotiations, being overwhelmed by the "compatibility" test. That wasn't just selling my V-card; that was signing up for a whole other lifetime commitment.

The scariest part about the idea was that it *didn't* scare me.

What did that say about me? I stared at the floor of the shower, my hair falling in a wet curtain around my face. Was I so lonely, so desperate for family and belonging that I would consider getting knocked up by a stranger for money?

Sure, women were surrogates and egg donors and all sorts of things. I had the feeling, however, that Dominic Stone wasn't suggesting I simply be the, uh, incubator for his billion dollar corporate legacy.

And where exactly did Jacob Stone come into this?

The water ran cold as I stood there, lost in my thoughts. By the time I got out and reached for a thread-bare towel, I was shivering uncontrollably. With my hair wrapped up in a terrycloth turban, I snuggled under the covers and fell asleep, drained by the emotional and physical intensity of just an hour in the presence of the Stone brothers.

When I woke up, my hair had dried into a troll doll style, and I was starving. I ate a bowl of cereal while checking my email at the tiny kitchen table, naked. Milk dribbled down my bare chest when I saw an email from Dom.

I couldn't help but wonder what kind of message a drop-dead billionaire would send after tag-teaming a strange woman in his office.

It was a deceptively simple email, but it flooded my heart with warmth as clicking on it prompted my screen to fill with fireworks and butterflies.

Dominic Stone made me come.

Then he made me laugh.

As my mother would have said, he's a keeper.

The thought of my parents saddened me, and I clicked on a folder where I had a bunch of family photos scanned and stored. I opened up a picture of my parents holding me in their arms. I must have been about a year old, and my image was blurred from my attempt to escape.

I'd always been in a hurry to grow up, get away, and for what? To be alone? My throat tightened.

Shit. What a Debbie downer I was being. I frowned. Weren't orgasm endorphins supposed to last longer?

I returned to my browser to see a new email from Dom. My heart thudded as I opened it. No fireworks this time, just an invitation to dinner the next evening. A frisson of *something* fizzled in the pit of my stomach.

It was safe to say that the Stone brothers had made a dangerous impression on me.

～

"So where do billionaires take their dates?" I teased as he led me to the waiting car.

"Hmmm, where do virgins like to go?"

I nearly tripped over my own feet, until he caught me.

"I'm beginning to think that you don't wear heels a lot." He grinned down at me in the early evening light, his olive skin burnished gold by the setting sun. That reminded me…

"How are you so dark and your brother is so blonde?"

His driver shut the door, enclosing us in the cool quiet of his limousine. Dom lifted up a bottle of champagne the same color as my short dress. I shook my head.

"Simple," he said as he put the wine back. "He's adopted."

Well, that would certainly make the whole "sex together, sort of" thing easier, I thought to myself. "So your grandfather's will—"

"Puts it all on me. I'm biologically an only child. But you understand what that's like."

A polite snort escaped me. "I think being fabulously wealthy might cushion the loneliness."

He arched an eyebrow at me. "Not if you wondered if all your friends were bought or rented."

I hadn't thought about it that way. "But you had your brother."

"As much as anyone *can* have Jake. Ah, here we are."

I looked out the window. We were at an old amusement park by the beach, a popular destination for tourists and families. Right now, it was deserted.

"It's closed," I pointed out.

"Not for us."

Oh. The power of money. We both looked down at my hazardous heels and the satin dress that stopped three inches above my knees. I wasn't dressed for this kind of date, but the intense, hopeful look on his face silenced my protests.

Two hours later, I was hoarse and dizzy, but we hadn't graduated past the kiddie rides. Dom found fiendish glee in ramming into me with a bumper car, and insisted on being my personal safety bar on the tilt and whirl.

After we gave up on the mini golf course, Dom checked his watch. Then he turned to me with those dark eyes that made me as breathless as the rides did.

"Walk on the beach?" he said, offering me his arm.

I could only nod. We walked toward the beach. It was more crowded here than at the amusement park; in my head I told myself that while he could buy out the park for the evening, he probably couldn't commandeer public property just to impress a date.

No, that wasn't fair of me. I shook the thought out of my head as I held on to his arm for balance and slipped off my heels.

"What's not fair?" he asked.

I *really* had to stop doing that! His expression was curious but not angry or concerned. He took my shoes and dangled them from one hand while he led me across the sand with the other.

The ocean was dark and shimmering before us, the sand cold on my feet.

"I was just thinking," I explained as we walked. "You didn't need to go to all this trouble. I'm, um, kind of a sure thing." It was obviously a joke, but I still hoped he couldn't see my blush in the moonlight.

"Evie, I want *you* to be sure." He squeezed my hand as he steered me away from where the tide licked the beach.

I was. Wasn't I?

Dom's wealth definitely made him more attractive, but was I being too mercenary? If I was honest with myself, I wouldn't be so eager to give up my V-card to a random computer engineer or truck driver if they had responded to my ad.

Then again, Dominic Stone was the only person who sent me an intelligent, courteous response—without a dick pic. That alone put him in a different league.

It also wasn't just about my virginity, anymore.

We'd stopped walking. Dom still held my hand but was peering at me like a puzzle he was trying to figure out.

"You don't have to impress me," I said, "that's all I meant. You're pretty… impressive already."

Dominic chuckled and shook his head as a popping noise interrupted us. He held our joined hands to the sky and pointed. "Look."

Fireworks exploded in the sky above us. They whistled and shimmered, in starburst patterns of changing color and twinkling waterfalls of light.

"Email just isn't enough," he murmured close to my ear. "Sorry, no butterflies."

The dancing sparks were so beautiful and so close, I could swear I felt their heat on my upturned face. My eyes closed briefly as he kissed my neck. "You do know how to woo a girl, Mister Stone."

"I like to have the upper hand in negotiations."

I turned to look him in the eye. Behind his confidence was the very real awareness that I could easily say no—to all of it. Fear of my rejection was the only chink in his armor that I could see.

"Why me?" I whispered. "I'm just… me."

"Exactly. It's 'just you.' There's something about you." His forehead creased, and he traced a line down the bridge of my nose. "I hate that you're alone. I feel like you need me. Need us."

Did I? Could I?

From the moment the auction idea had crossed my mind, I knew that it would be hard to hang on to my inhibitions, or even the ladylike instincts that fought blindly against my sexual curiosity. But this…

"I'll take care of you, Evie," he promised. "Both of you."

Peaceful warmth grew in my chest at the idea of cradling a baby to me, its soft mouth searching for sustenance and tiny little fingers wrapping around mine.

Oh god, I had to be insane for even considering this.

"I'd never give up my child," I blurted out.

"I wouldn't ask you to. A child needs its mother. Don't you wish you still had yours?" he asked.

I froze, momentarily forgetting that I'd discussed my background in our emails. And he had his "reports." Even if I was seriously going to think about this, there were so many questions, so many hypotheticals.

He pressed his thumb to the frown building between my eyebrows. "Stop it, Evie. Stop overthinking it. Why don't we just start with the first part, and see where it goes?"

The first part? Oh right, my virginity.

"Are you…" I trailed off, not certain what to say.

Was he sure about this? Good for the money? Going to be gentle? Clean? Protected? Planning to rock my world again?

I shook my head, trying to throw off all the questions and fears. If I'd been bold—or stupid—enough to place the ad, then I'd have to trust myself to go through with the consequences. I was lucky to have someone like Dominic Stone respond. At least I knew he was on the up and up.

Something occurred to me. It was like being struck by lightning.

"Would you consider a loan?"

He narrowed his eyes. "You mean, give you the money you need for nothing in return?"

I blushed. "Well, you *are* a billionaire."

Clearing his throat, he looked off into the distance. "I don't have as much power as you think. A lot of it is controlled by my grandfather and his lawyer. That's why I want to claim my inheritance, free and clear—so I have independence and can make decisions, changes to the business."

"Changes to your life."

He nodded, his jaw tight. It was hard to imagine a man like Dom Stone powerless, but I realized that in many ways he was. We were both trapped, in a way. Maybe we did need each other.

"Dom?" I squeezed his hand.

He looked back at me, his gaze clearing of the mist of self-reflection. "Hmmm?"

"Take me? Take me to bed. Take me to the car. Take me—somewhere."

His eyes darkened with anticipation and lust, sending a tremor through me. The fireworks above us had ended, but the ones between us were about to begin.

JAKE

I promised Dom I wouldn't butt in. I *promised*.

But somebody had to coordinate the well-compensated amusement park staff, and if it just so happened that I spied on my brother and Evie a little… then, well, that was just too bad.

"She's still on the fence, Jake," he'd warned me earlier. "We don't want to scare her off."

I snorted loudly when he said that. "You were there for that scene in the office, right?" My dick hardened with the memory of the sweet, peachy way she tasted.

Only Dominic Stone could seethe with iciness. "Don't," he snapped. "She's the one. *Don't* fuck it up for us."

"'Us' being you and me, or you and her?" His silence made me nervous. "Dude, we're in this together, right?" We had been a team for nearly twenty years.

I was a dumb, punk-ass kid when I was brought to the house to meet Asa Stone. The obvious wealth impressed the shit out of me—or it would have if I hadn't been too intimidated to let loose on one of his solid gold toilets.

It wasn't until a lot later that I realized adolescent boys in the foster care system weren't usually adopted by rich old dudes.

But Grandad Stone wasn't a pedophile. He just wanted to live in another century.

Believe it or not, he arranged to adopt me to be a companion to his orphaned grandson, Dominic. Seriously, it was like buying a friend for Richie Rich! I couldn't believe he could even get away with it, but money talked and ethics walked.

To say that it didn't go well at first would be an understatement.

Basically I did everything I could to spend the old man's money and fuck with the staff. I ordered an expensive dirt bike and rode it in the house. I had pizza delivered three times a day, then left the debris everywhere for the maids to clean up. I even jerked off in the pool and laughed as they tried to scoop out the splooge.

Mostly, though, I made fun of the sad, dark-eyed little rich boy who'd been forced to share his wing of the mansion.

At first Dominic ignored me, humiliated by the realization that his grandfather had bought a brother for him. Shit, I would be embarrassed, too—if I wasn't so happy that for once in my short life I'd landed on my ass instead of my head. His emo brooding and sulking didn't bother me, as long as he stayed out of my way.

One day, he didn't stay out of my way.

The tension between us blew up once Grandad tried to spank me after a particularly hefty credit card bill arrived. No shit, the man tried to take his *cane* to me.

Like I said, though—old-fashioned, not kinky. In a rare display of defiance, Dom stopped him. Protected me.

Then, after we escaped back to our rooms, he beat the shit out of me himself.

The next day, we were both moving slower, but a mutual respect had been forged. Our truce over the next few years turned into a kind of friendly competition in how to be an asshole.

Cheating on tests together, check.

Volunteering together to boost our college applications, check.

Trying out for the football team together, check.

Fucking the head cheerleader together… check!

It hadn't happened a lot, but enough to make us the topic of quiet gossip. Instead of people being creeped out, though, guys were jealous as fuck and girls were lining up to take off their panties for us—as long as we didn't tell anyone, of course.

Yeah, right. The girls were always the first to spread the rumors, soon after they spread their legs.

Our twenties went by in a blur of babes and business school. We each had our strengths; his was the latter. In an uninspired fit of disobedience, I dropped out of our MBA program and enlisted in the army.

Joining up just to irritate somebody is not the best strategy, just so you know. I'd gotten a bit too used to the cushy life, so basic training beat the shit out of me. But after a while, I discovered I liked the structure; liked the feeling of belonging and camaraderie.

I also liked fucking around on leave, which shouldn't have surprised anyone. What did surprise Grandad and Dom was the surprise baby I came home to on my next leave. *Fuck my life.*

The second I saw her I was a goner. Her mother, I'm ashamed to say, was pretty forgettable. But the baby, my daughter? Well, the first time Stella held my finger it was like looking into the sun.

So, home to finish the MBA and join the family business so I could support my little girl and her mother, who thankfully didn't have any interest in rekindling our fire. It was back to business in every way, except for seeing Stella on weekends.

Other than my daughter, some new tattoos, a few nightmares, and my ability to Ranger roll the fuck out of all my clothes, my service time could have been a figment of my imagination.

Fast-forward a few years, which I discovered goes by fast when you have a kid, and Grandad drops a cancer diagnosis on us.

As if that weren't bad enough, he let me know that the amended terms of his last will and testament shut my daughter out as a potential "heir." *Motherfucker.* Dom told me not to worry, that he'd take care of it.

Now, I leaned against a concrete wall separating the beach and the sidewalk, and watched Dominic reel Evie in.

I was jealous; I could admit it. I just didn't know whom I was really jealous of. We had an understanding —"it's not gay if your dicks don't touch"—but I'd never seen Dom be so possessive of a woman he'd just met.

Evie was pretty hot, though. She had this thing going on where she was timid one minute and a raging cock slut the next. She probably didn't even know she was doing it.

At the moment, my own jeans were getting tight as I watched her trail her fingers over Dom's crotch. His back straightened like a steel rod had replaced his spine, and for a few seconds I thought something had gone wrong.

The way he suddenly wrapped himself around her like a boa constrictor was both a relief and a warning. Evie was not going to be a casual affair.

I palmed myself through my jeans in the dark as he lowered his head to her neck. In the night air, her moans were audible and her shivers authentic. I swallowed, saliva filling my mouth. After having fun with her at the office, I was dying to get another taste of that pretty pink pussy.

"Dominic, please? We can't—" she gasped loudly. "Not here." Her gaze swept around, but she didn't spot me in the shadows.

He growled something into her ear, and her eyes closed. The expression on her face was concealed, though, as my brother kissed her long and hard. His hands glided over her, stopping in places to squeeze her softest and most tender parts. *Lucky sonofabitch.*

She was probably soaking wet by now, I thought to myself. *Come on, Dom, what are you waiting for?* My body throbbed in sympathetic arousal as I willed his hand to fly between her thighs.

"Oh! *Ahhh!*"

Bullseye. My hands curled into fists at my side as I imagined the slickness of her arousal on my own fingers. My touch would be less forgiving than his, my need more demanding.

I closed my eyes, trying to remember the exact color and taste of her pussy. When I opened them, licking my lips, Dom had tugged her back to the car and was closing the door behind them. The driver stood about twenty feet away, reading a magazine.

"Hey," I said. "They don't want to go home?"

He raised an eyebrow at me. "Not yet, I guess."

A muffled thump came from inside the car. I could only guess what made it. How far had they gotten? The trusted family retainer and I shared a knowing smirk.

"Is the screen up?" I asked.

He nodded, tilting his head at me. "Whatcha thinking?"

I fished out the keys to my truck and tossed them to him. "I'll drive them home."

The liveried chauffeur held my gaze for a long minute then grinned. "Want my cap?"

"Shit, no. You might have cooties."

"As you wish, sir." He bowed slightly, giving me the finger, then whapped his thigh with his rolled-up magazine and headed in the direction of my truck.

Oh, this was going to be fun.

EVIE

*D*ominic Stone's tongue was in my mouth when the car began moving. We were both lucky I hadn't bit down in surprise.

"Wha—?" He pulled back and spun toward the front seat. Rapped on the privacy window thingy. "Smith!"

The car was picking up speed, so I sat back and put on my seatbelt. *Safety first.*

I pressed the backs of my fingers against my burning cheeks. We slowed down a little as the screen made a whirring noise and Dom talked to the driver, but I just stared out the window beside me. The lights of the park were shutting off, like someone dropping a big black blanket over it.

I'd told Dom to take me. *Begged* him to take me. I was going to be his, but I was a little glad that the moment had been interrupted. Losing my v-card in the back seat of a car after a date to an amusement park would be kind of cliché, though. At least it wasn't prom.

When he sat back beside me, he wasn't nearly as

annoyed as I thought he'd be. He actually had a smile on his face.

"What?" I asked.

"Nothing." He chuckled. "It's nothing. Would you like to see my apartment?"

"Not your mansion?" I joked.

Dom frowned. "I don't want you to meet Grandad yet."

I froze. "Oh."

"No! I just don't want *you* to have to deal with *him*," he backtracked. "And I want you all to myself."

A phrase that Annie had used once popped into my head. "So you're taking me back to your 'pussy pad?'"

Dom's eyes blackened to obsidian. He crowded close to me, his spicy scent in my nose and his voice rough in my ear. "Do you know how fucking sexy it is to hear you say that?"

"Pad?" I whispered.

Of course I knew he meant my hooha reference, but I was quickly discovering how much fun it could be to play with a man like this.

He was so intense, so direct and dark. There was vulnerability in him, though, like a little boy forced to grow up too fast. Maybe that's exactly what had happened, though. Part of me wanted to put his head in my lap and stroke his hair with sweeping, soothing motions.

Another part of me just wanted his head. In. My. Lap.

"Those sweet, sinful lips," he murmured against my neck, "saying dirty things is making me hard as a rock."

I shivered, remembering the musky taste of his thick cock. Listening to him was doing a number on my girly parts, too. Turning a powerful man on was, well, a powerful feeling. *I could get used to this*, I thought to myself.

His lips curved into a smile as he kissed me, his palms warm on my thighs as he crept under the hem of my dress again. My nipples tightened exquisitely in anticipation, but self-consciousness made me inch back.

"Nuh uh," I chided. "Not until we get to the hooha house."

Dominic stilled before falling back against the smooth leather seat with a groan. "Fuck, even *that* is sexy. And utterly ridiculous."

Slouched in the back of the limo, I could have pointed out that his erection jutted out of his pants in a similarly "ridiculous" way, but my mouth was too dry to get the words out. I was also acutely aware of the way his pinky finger still stroked the side of my knee.

Were we slowing down? It seemed like we were slowing down.

His little finger left my knee and found my hand, wrapping itself around my own pinky. He tugged, getting my attention.

"I'm going to taste every inch of your skin, suck it until it plumps up for me," he said quietly. "Now that I've already felt you on my tongue, on my fingers, I can't wait to slide my cock into you."

"Oh." My voice was small as I imagined it.

He shook his head slightly, as if waking from a daze. "You have no idea what you do to me, do you? I would pay a thousand times over what I've already promised for the privilege of your pussy."

I swallowed—sort of. The seams of the concrete thwipped rhythmically under the tires as we shot down the freeway toward downtown. "Will it hurt?"

"Not by the time I'm done with you."

"When will that be?"

"Never." With a click, he undid my seatbelt and hauled me onto his lap.

Breathless from both the sudden movement and the declaration, my hands went to his chest like kneading little kitten paws. I leaned into him as we turned a corner.

"Dom! This isn't safe."

"Fuck safety," he growled, palming the curve of my lower belly possessively.

$\sim$

*I*t could have been five minutes or fifty before the car finally stopped. His ravenous kisses had depleted me of oxygen; his caresses stripped me of sense.

"We're here."

I looked out the window at the underground parking lot. Fluorescent lights glinted off of luxury cars and allowed for no dark corners.

The car door opening startled me, piercing our hazy bubble of backseat lust.

Jacob Stone leaned his head in, his arm braced against the roof of the limo. "We're here," he echoed his brother's announcement.

My mouth fell open. "Were you there the whole time?"

He smirked at me, his blue eyes blazing. "Define 'there.'"

"Or 'the whole time,'" Dom muttered, making my head whip around to look at him. "Out you get, Evie."

My gaze went from Dominic to Jacob. What did this mean? *Both of them? Again?* My insides flipped at the idea, but not in a bad way.

"Out I get," I repeated faintly.

The butterflies in my belly fluttered wildly as I walked between the two men to the elevator bank. As we rose, the weightless sensation in my body was not just due to the speedy ascent. I squeezed my thighs together. The heat of the brothers' bodies on either side of mine both stifled and comforted me.

We were all silent as the elevator door opened directly into a massive apartment. Dom took my hand and led me into the marble-floored foyer.

"Shoes, Jake!" he reminded his brother. Jake rolled his eyes before toeing off his shoes.

I stepped out of my heels, my feet immediately soothed by the cool, hard floor. Immediately I felt more delicate, uncertain—as though my shoes had boosted my confidence as well as my height. When I tilted my head back to look up at Dom, his large hand cradled my jaw, brushing my apprehension away with every sweep of his thumb.

Tingles. Sizzles. Vibrations. I felt them all inside me, like a fizzing candy dissolving on my tongue.

When Jake's hand landed on my lower back, I reflexively arched into it.

"We got you," he assured me as he swept my hair off my neck and dropped a kiss there.

Oh my god. I stumbled forward a little. "I can't—not for the first time—"

There was crazy, and then there was just outright insane. No matter what secret fantasies I might have, or what smutty stories I might read in secret, I never expected my first time to be with more than one person.

In the back of my head, I thought to myself, "If my daughter asks me someday about my first time, I can't tell her I got a two-for-one special!"

Jake clapped his hand over his mouth as he barked out a laugh.

Oh crap. I said that part out loud.

Dom glared over my head at his brother and took my hand. "You don't have to."

My head spun.

"Look at me, Evie." I did. His gaze steadied me. "It's just us right now, okay? No expectations." At my raised eyebrow, he chuckled and added, "Okay, there are *some* expectations, but I will never hurt you. I promise you that."

I believed him.

He took me into a cavernous living room, where Jake flopped onto a modern leather couch. With my hand still in Dom's, he then led me down a hallway to a large bedroom filled with dark wood and creamy fabrics. The massive bed was unmade, and the curtains wide open to let the starlight in.

"I left the bathroom light on," Dom murmured to himself. The strip of light from his ensuite stretched across the light carpet like an arrow pointing to the bed.

"Do you want to turn it off?" I asked, hoping for a little more darkness to hide my body.

"Not a chance, beautiful." He squeezed my hip. "If I had my way I'd put on every light in the place so I could see every inch of you."

A squeak escaped me.

"But I won't, because I want you to be comfortable."

We both smiled as our eyes met. "Well, as comfortable as this situation allows, anyhow."

"Then keep touching me, Dom. Please touch me." His hands made me nervous but his gaze excited me, his admiration swelling my confidence. Or was it the other way around? Just being with him made me feel like I was on a rocking boat, needing to look at the horizon to steady myself.

"Oh baby, this is just the beginning."

He pulled my hands to the buttons of his shirt, urging me to undo them. My fingers only trembled a little, freezing briefly as he reached around to unzip the back of my floaty little dress, all the way down over my ass. Standing close to each other, my dress fell off my shoulders, but not to the floor. His mouth devoured me, the crisp hairs on his chest brushing against my chest as he held me close.

Suddenly I felt an urgent need, a primal desire to have his naked skin against mine. All of it.

He groaned as I pushed his shirt off. "Yes," he hissed. When he stepped away from me, my dress fell to the carpet. I'd borrowed Annie's bra and thong set for the evening, and judging from the lust in his eyes it was a good decision.

"Fucking gorgeous." Dominic reached out and shoved the cups of the white lace bra down to fill his hands with my breasts. At first I was taken aback, then aching arousal zapped through me as he tweaked my nipples.

He pulled me toward the bed, but instead of pushing me onto it, he sat on the edge with me standing before him, and reached around to unhook my bra. My hands went to his bare shoulders to steady myself. I was now totally naked, except for the lacy dental floss between my ass cheeks.

Dom palmed the ass cheeks in question, and I blushed all over as his thumb ran underneath the stretchy waistband. "Did you wear this for me?"

I nodded, blushing a little as he traced the waistband around to my navel. He pulled down the thong, letting it sit over my hips and just above the path to my swollen, seeping core.

Silently he bent forward and kissed my belly, right there between my hips. "I want to make this swell," he said in a hoarse voice. "I want to put a baby there." His tongue traced invisible patterns in my skin, his hands hot and possessive as they moved over me.

His fervor shocked me. And it turned me on as he closed his lips over one of my aching nipples.

"Ahhh!"

I cried out. Jolts of unfamiliar sensations, both sexual and maternal, went through me as he nursed. He suckled hard, giving me no retreat, no pause, demanding and hot. How was it possible to feel all these strange things, all at once? I barely noticed that he was clinging on to me with only his mouth, as his hands went to the front of his slacks.

In a few brief, dizzying motion, he had me on my back the bed. He tugged the thong down my thighs and threw it aside, before yanking off the rest of his own clothes.

He crawled onto the bed, between my splayed thighs, kneeling up and fisting his cock as it pointed firmly up to the ceiling. "You're dripping, Evie," he said. "I can see it. You're so fucking wet."

Reflexively I moved to close my legs, but he dropped

down to his elbows and nudged his head between my thighs. With his hands clamped over my legs I was unable to move, other than arching my back and screaming when he licked me from the bottom of my slit to the hard bud of my clit.

A curse burst forth from me, as earthy and sensuous as I felt.

"Yes, Evie, yes. I'm going to fuck you so good. I'm going to have every inch of you."

Lust overtook my heart and brain as I nodded my assent. *Oh god, yes.*

I hadn't realized how close to the edge I was until my pussy began clenching around his tongue. Vibrations began in my center, radiating like the hum of a tuning fork.

With his broad thumbs he spread my lower lips apart to expose my throbbing clit. I panted as he lightly poked at the sensitive flesh with the tip of his tongue. A keening sound leaked from me, like the flood of juices that he lapped up.

"You're going to feel me everywhere, Evie."

I already did. I closed my eyes. "Oh my god, Dom. Please!"

"*Everywhere*," he promised. Illicit fantasies and sultry images flew through my head as my orgasm splintered me.

"Me too," I heard, but Dom's tongue was buried in my pussy. *Wasn't it?*

My eyes flew open and my head flopped to the side. Jake stood in the doorway with his erection in his hands. Shock stilled my body while my insides pulsated.

Jake's tanned, nude body mesmerized me—the rippling waves of his washboard abs, the surprising tattoos climbing up his muscular arms. Where Dominic was dark and sleek like a panther, Jake was like a lazy lion flexing his power in the sun. I licked my lips as he approached.

My walls still fluttered, spasms of pleasure penetrating my consciousness. Dom growled something at his brother, but I was only aware of the heat and hardness on me, over me, beside me—and my own body still open and aching.

Maybe that was his strategy the whole time—a sexual sleight of hand, distracting me with misdirection at the moment I was most vulnerable and dazed.

So it was that I reached out and curiously wrapped my hand around Jake's cock at the same time that Dom moved above. He filled me, piercing my hymen and filling my virgin cunt until there was barely room in me for my own panting breaths.

"So tight!" Dom's eyes and mine both widened with shock, and Jake groaned as I reflexively squeezed him.

"Oh my god!"

"Evie!" Dom's harsh tone focused my attention back on him. He braced himself above me, his shoulders tensed and his arms like marble. Sweat beaded on his forehead, and he licked his lips and nodded. "It's just us, okay? Only me inside you right now, I promise."

Jake whined with disappointment when I let go of him. Dom withdrew a little then drove into me again. And again. The foreign weight and presence in my body felt less like an invasion, and more like a homecoming.

I hadn't realized how empty I was until he filled me up.

"More," I heard myself saying—begging, without even knowing what it was that I wanted.

Dom's thrusts sped up, the force driving me inch by inch over the bed toward Jake—by accident or by plan, I had no idea. Perhaps it was all really my idea, my fantasies driving us, because the coil inside me unraveled like a Slinky, another orgasm washing over me. *Had I even stopped coming the first time?*

"Fuck, baby, you're squeezing me so hard," Dom gritted out. "Get ready. Here it comes! I'm gonna fill you now."

My womb contracted along with the rest of my body as the thought of him shooting his seed inside me. A wet rush of pleasure overcame me with each of his grunts and pulsing sprays. It was *so much*, yet not enough.

"More," I croaked, my gaze meeting Jake's above my head.

He nodded.

I looked to Dom again, anticipation making my mouth dry.

"You sure?" he asked.

I nodded.

"'Kay," Dom grunted as he finished flooding me. "Fuck, Evie. You're just—*fuck*!" He was speechless as he alternately tensed and trembled against me. Slowly he pulled out, leaning back on his heels to eye my flushed, moist body with satisfaction. "Now?"

I nodded.

My lips parted in welcome as Jake stuffed his cock into my mouth. As his weeping tip touched the back of my palate, my eyes watered. His hips jerked.

"Oh Christ, I can't stop. Sorry, Evie, fuck fuck *fuck*!"

My nostrils flared as cum poured down my throat. I gulped and gurgled. I inhaled. I tried not to choke, tilting my head back further. Jake hissed as I swallowed around his sensitive glans.

"Once more, baby." With determination, Dom caught the semen dripping from my hole and rubbed it into me. His thick fingers shoved it back in my pussy at the same time as Jake spurted in my mouth.

As Dom massaged our combined juices into my ripe, aching clit, Jake pulled up to paint my mouth with the last drips of his creamy seed.

Their attentions overwhelmed me, tossing me over the edge again. I shuddered through yet another, smaller climax, with Jake's salty taste on my lips and my belly full of cum.

As far as losing my virginity went, I was apparently an overachiever.

DOMINIC

"*J*esus fucking Christ." I bent over, winded and sweaty.

"Pussy," Jake coughed out under his breath.

The last quarter-mile of our friendly run on the beach had turned into a kind of death match, which I clearly had lost. The third time I stumbled, I let myself fall onto the sand and tried to get my heartbeat down.

Actually, my heart had been racing and irregular for two—no, three weeks now, ever since meeting Evie.

Since tasting Evie. Since having Evie.

Yeah, I was a pussy.

I couldn't stop thinking about her. The cynical part of me thought she'd disappear as soon as she got the confirmation from the bank about her debts being paid off. She had every right, after all.

But two days after all the transfers were finalized, she showed up at the office with a picnic lunch for us. Not a tongue-in-cheek, smother her with peanut butter and jelly and call her a sandwich, but she actually had a tote bag with cheese and crusty bread, fresh fruit and a small bottle of wine.

"What are you doing here?" I frowned, flicking to the calendar on my phone. Was there a problem with the payments?

"Nope! I just wanted to say thanks." Her smile filled the room. "And I think you need to take a lunch break."

I really didn't, but I wasn't about to tell her that and risk running her off. In the end, we found a park nearby and spread our feast out on a folded up sheet she'd wrapped the wine bottle in.

We ate. Kissed. Ate. Kissed. Drank. Kissed. Ultimately, I think I savored *her* more than the food she'd brought. But what people said was true—everything *did* taste better outside.

The noontime wine made her a little wobbly, so I took her home in a cab before heading back to work. Her friend Annie took over in the lobby of their little walk-up apartment building. Wide eyes and hushed whispers followed me out the door.

Evie's friend gasped. "Is he the one?" I heard her ask.

I hadn't needed to hear the answer for my stroll to turn into a strut. I put on my sunglasses and grinned like a lunatic all the way back to the office.

Now, this morning's jog had turned into a run, and Jake had left me in the dust. We'd always been competitive, but today my brother wasn't letting the chip on his shoulder weigh him down.

"What's wrong with you?" I asked, wishing I had a bottle of water.

Jake wouldn't sit, instead pacing back and forth with his arms crossed tightly over his chest. "I haven't seen Stella in two weeks."

"Damn. Why?"

Back. Forth. Back. Forth. "Fuck if I know." He muttered something about his ex and some family emergency a couple of states over.

"I wish Grandad got how much you love your daughter," I thought out loud.

Jake was a mass of contradictions. Brawny and built like a Midwestern farm boy, his muscles were big and his ideas small. He was the kind of guy that constantly surprised you, even surprising himself at the same time. Like with Stella. Admittedly I hadn't spent a lot of time with the baby, but Jake tended to wear his heart on his sleeve—when he was wearing a shirt, anyhow.

At the moment, his tanned torso was gleaming in the bright sunlight. The dude was a show-off, even still wearing his dog tags despite being out of the service.

He snorted. "No shit. But then you—we—wouldn't have met Evie."

The idea rattled me, but I still felt bad on his behalf. It wasn't his fault he knocked up a total bitch. Well, okay, it *was*, but mistakes happen—not that he'd call Stella a mistake. Either way, Grandad was being too rigid about the whole inheritance slash legacy thing.

And I—we—*did* meet Evie. Biblically.

That first time was still the only time that the three of us had been together, in any way. The next morning Evie and I had woken in my bed to find Jake long gone, and her phone blowing up with calls from her friend. She was too flustered to be up for some morning sex. She was also sore "down there."

That was understandable.

Since our picnic, we'd somehow fallen into a pattern of lunch a few times a week. I took her to a fancy place for dinner, where she looked around with eyes the size of the gilded charger plates before focusing them on me.

"I can't be here."

I nearly choked on the martini I'd brought over from the bar where we'd waited for our table. "What?"

She shifted in her seat and methodically picked up every item on the table. "This is too much."

Looking around, I didn't understand what she meant. "Is the place too big? Too noisy? Too—"

"Too expensive."

"So?" I frowned.

"I'm not dressed for this kind of place," she whisper-hissed at me.

Well, sure, she wasn't dripping in diamonds or designer clothes, but she wasn't exactly wearing a clown suit either. Everything about her was simple and subtle, which was one of the things I lo—liked about her.

Now she blushed with embarrassment, as I openly looked up and down her body, from the silver hoops in her ears to the flouncy hem of her black dress. Her legs were bare, and she wore the same heels that she'd worn to the "interview" and our date at the amusement park.

It only occurred to me then that she might only have one pair of good heels. With legs like hers, that would be a fucking tragedy that I'd have to remedy.

"You look fine," I assured her.

A huffing, grumbling noise came from deep inside her throat. "Thanks." The tone of her voice told me she wasn't actually grateful.

She picked up the menu and glanced through it,

before placing it carefully on the table. "Excuse me, please. I need to, uh…"

I barely had time to admire the shapely curves of her ass in her dress as she scurried away.

After seven minutes, I realized that it was an escape, not a bathroom break. Now it was my turn to make a frustrated noise as I got up and found the ladies room.

I opened the door at the same time that a middle-aged woman—who *was* wearing diamonds and designer clothes, naturally—came out.

"Oh!"

"Sorry. I'm looking for my—"

She looked down her nose job at me. "If that's your wife crying in there then you'd better go apologize."

"For what?" *Shit, what had Evie told her?*

"For everything. Anything. Being a man is a good place to start." She sniffed with contempt and stalked out to the main dining room.

With a deep sigh, I went in. "Evie? Please come out, honey."

I heard the telltale sound of a toilet roll being pulled and a nose being blown. The restroom was almost as fancy and romantic as the restaurant. Everything sparkled, including Evie's eyes when she emerged. Her nose was red and tears welled up in her eyes, threatening to overflow.

Goddammit.

"C'mere." I held out my hand and tried to wait patiently, like she was a wounded animal. Patience was not my strong suit.

I was about to reach for her when she stepped toward me, her heels clicking on the tile. When she was close enough, I pulled her into my arms and squeezed another huffing, grumbling noise out of her.

"I'm sorry," she mumbled.

"No, *I'm* sorry. We'll go. I didn't know it bothered you that much." Designer nose job lady was right—I was a stupid, insensitive man.

She looked at my chest and nodded silently. I nudged her chin up so I could look her in the eye.

"Would it help if I fucked you here?"

Her gaze flew to the long granite countertop where glass vessel sinks bloomed like a row of flowers, then looked at me with horror. "You're joking."

"I'm deadly serious." My dick was hardening in my pants as I said it. I didn't want her crying as we walked out of here. I'd rather she be smiling.

"Somebody could come in."

My lips touched her ear as I whispered, "That's part of the fun." A shiver wracked her curvy body. "You want to, don't you? You want to be naughty and risk it."

She let out a little moan as my nose dragged down her neck. Then I moaned when my wandering hand found her damp panties. *Thank fuck she wasn't wearing one of those spanky girdle things*, I thought to myself.

I kissed her, gently at first, then harder and with more hunger, as if we knew that time was not on our side. I teased her center, tracing the edges of her panties, trying to get her to beg for my fingers.

She undid my pants with trembling fingers, breaking our kiss to glance at the door. Her gasp as she pulled out my rock hard cock made me chuckle.

"It's like your first time, every time. Isn't it, Evie?" Her reactions were so innocent, but inside I knew she was burning with desire. She had a raging sexual curiosity, but I could tell she was embarrassed by her emerging needs. "You want my cock, don't you?" I asked her.

In response, she wrapped her fingers around me and squeezed. *Impertinent wench.* Now was *not* the time to hear Grandad's voice in my head. I shook it out, blinking at her, my hands going to her shoulders.

"Get on your knees," I commanded roughly.

She did. Her nipples stuck out against the fabric of her dress, and the skirt tightened around her thighs as she knelt before me. Still she held my dick, which was throbbing and eager.

"Suck my cock, Evie."

With only a fraction of hesitation, she leaned forward and tried to get her mouth around my erection.

"Fuck, yes!" My hands went into her hair as she bobbed up and down, trying to taste all of me.

Warm. Wet. Soft. Firm. Rough.

"Do you want me to come in your mouth, baby?" In the heavenly haven of her mouth, I was getting close —fast.

She shook her head, my cock brushing against her back molars and making me grunt.

"Get up. Take off your panties."

Again, only a slight pause before she obeyed. She stepped out of them and held them from two fingers, looking around as if she wasn't sure what to do with them.

I knew exactly what to do with Evie's wet panties.

Taking them from her, I briefly sniffed them before shoving them in my pocket. They created a bulge, but I was used to having a bulge in my pants.

I kissed her again, my body hot and straining toward release. I needed to be inside her—now. Twenty seconds ago would be even fucking better.

When I tested her with my finger, I found her slick and plump with arousal. Two fingers. Then three. Her pussy tried to suck me in and push me out at the same time.

"Dom!" she moaned against my mouth. "*Please.*"

There was the begging. A satisfied smile stretched my mouth at the same time as we both registered a noise outside the door.

Shit!

I shoved her until her back hit the door and my hands braced against it, keeping it closed.

Evie yelped in surprise as someone behind the door pushed back, trying to get in. With my considerable strength, I kept them out.

"Sorry, ma'am! There was an unfortunate incident, that we're just taking care of right now!" I called out.

The pressure on the other side of the door eased. "How long will it be?"

I reached down to pull up Evie's dress. "Not long," I said, looking at her gorgeous creamy thighs and the dewy patch of hair between them.

"What are you—*ah!*" She sucked in a surprised breath as I hauled her up, my hands clamped around her curves.

We both exhaled harshly as I impaled her on my cock. A thud sounded out as I pressed her into the door, and her dress rasped against the wood as she moved up and down with each thrust.

"Is she gone?" Evie panted.

"I don't. Fucking. Care," I grunted back, my body taut and hurtling toward release. "God, your pussy is so fucking tight. *Every. Time!*"

It was like taking her virginity every time I entered her—so tight and hot.

I tried to move one hand—to tease her clit, tweak her nipple, anything—but her luscious hourglass figure needed my undivided attention, and both hands to keep her on my cock as long as possible.

"I didn't know I could do this," she confessed, her chin dropping to my shoulder and her husky voice in my ear. "I always imagined I was too heavy, too—"

"Shut up and let me fuck you."

My sassy girl bit my earlobe in response. Burning heat seared my dick, but also my thighs and glutes. Sweat broke out on my body, with the effort and the knowledge that I was seconds away from flooding her lovely body with my life-giving seed.

I ground against her pubic bone with each thrust, until she was biting her lip to keep in her wails. "Come, Evie. Come with me," I ordered.

She made a high-pitched noise that threatened to become a scream before I covered her mouth with mine. Her slick walls quivered around me, gripping my cock rhythmically until I was unable to do anything but pour into her.

"*Ungh ungh fuck!* Yes! Take it, Evie. *Take it!*"

I came so hard I felt like my cum was shooting out of my spine, straight up into her. She whimpered with every hot pulse, until I was left sweaty and boneless with satisfaction.

My muscles protested as I lowered her carefully to the floor.

"No, stay in me!" she begged, trying to wrap her legs around my hips.

"I can't, baby. We can't stay here."

She nodded as I kissed her. I hated having to withdraw from her, but at forty dollars an entrée, I was guessing most patrons here expected an available ladies room.

Hopefully they wouldn't mind that it smelled like sex.

We both had smiles on our faces as we left the restaurant—and a generous gratuity, despite not ordering anything. It reminded me of an old dirty joke.

"What did the leper say to the prostitute?" I asked Evie with a grin. She raised an eyebrow. "Keep the tip."

She was still giggling when the valet brought around the car.

That was the last time I took her somewhere so… conspicuous. She was much happier discovering hole in the wall family restaurants. One night she even insisted on making dinner in my apartment, since her "kitchen" was so tiny she suspected it had been salvaged from a Barbie dream house.

I tried to buy her some designer dresses, but was disappointed to discover that they didn't make anything in her size. She scolded me for even looking.

What kind of girl didn't want to be spoiled? Evie, apparently.

Paying off her debts was really all she'd wanted. She wasn't looking for a sugar daddy. I truly believed her when she confessed that signing up for that website was both a drunken mistake and an act of desperation.

Intoxicated by the scent of her skin, I confessed that going on the auction site wasn't exactly regular web surfing for me, either. I blamed Jake. She believed me.

Would she believe me if I told her I was falling for her?

"Dominic!" Jake's large fingers snapped in front of my face. "You listening to me?"

"Of course." *Not one bit.* I blinked at his hand as it waved before me. We'd been talking about his daughter, Stella, right?

"I just want a little time with her, you know?" He slid his old dog tags up and down on the chain, making a sound like a zipper.

"Yeah, I'm sure."

My body had cooled down from the run, my muscles starting to stiffen up a bit. I needed to get moving again.

"So it's okay with you?"

"Whatever you need, man. I support you one hundred percent."

Jake's whole body relaxed. His dog tags fell silent as he stopped anxiously tugging at them. "Awesome."

He did a few windmills with his arms then bounded down the path like Tigger. Whatever I'd just agreed to, it gave him a burst of happiness and energy.

I stretched out my quads and hamstrings quickly, careful not to face plant on the beach, then began jogging slowly behind him. I fucking hated running on sand, but Jake insisted on the challenge.

He was so far ahead of me already that I barely heard him when he turned back to me and yelled, "I promise I'll wear a condom, okay? One baby is enough for me. That's your territory, dude."

My stop was so sudden, it should have had

screeching sound effects accompanying it. My toes actually slid forward, smushing painfully against the front of my shoes.

"*What?*"

JAKE

"*T*his place is amazing!"

Something in me lightened at the sight of Evie's smile. It was so pure, so guileless. There was nothing fake or manipulative about her, unlike a lot of the women I'd known. I looked around, trying to see the place through her eyes.

We were in a dollhouse—almost literally. It was the company's first boutique toy store, and it was admittedly a big gamble. These days, when most kids had their eyes glued to a screen and with online shopping so easy, it was hard to see why a kid would choose to come here.

I still hoped they would.

The store was shaped like a star, with the tills in the middle. Each of the points stretching out had a different theme. One was a miniature play house, another was a science and technology lab. Then there was a zoo, a small-scale city, and the last one was empty—on purpose.

Evie strode over to the blank space, her long

sundress rippling behind her. "What are you putting in here?"

"Nothing, yet. Blocks. Cardboard boxes. Paper on the walls, maybe?"

She spun around in a circle, squinting her eyes. "So they can use their imaginations?"

"Yeah, that was the idea."

"This really is fantastic, Jake. You should be really proud of yourself. This was all you?"

My face grew hot. "Mostly." I laughed, sort of. "I guess a single dad without a kid—most of the time—has an imagination, too."

Her smile faded from delight into sympathy. Fuck, I *hated* that. I wasn't weak or needy, and I didn't need her big hazel eyes getting all moist and girly on me.

Time to end this pity party.

"Right now my imagination is telling me that you are wearing black panties under that dress."

She rolled her eyes and turned away to drift back to the central cash register. "Nice try," she said, but there was extra sway in her hips as she walked away.

Her silver flip-flops smacked at her heels as they peeped out from beneath the hem of her white flowy dress. She looked like an angel from the top of a Christmas tree.

In the past month or so, Evie had gone from virgin to vixen—at least according to Dominic. She still put on a shy, sardonic demeanor to the outside world, but was wild and curious in the bedroom.

She'd been the one to call *me* to ask about a date. Dom said he was okay with it, which surprised me a little. But whatever. I didn't answer his calls or texts in the last two days, not wanting any of his "helpful" advice or dating "tips."

I had my own style with women, and I didn't need tall, dark, and *Dominic* questioning everything. So far, Evie hadn't had any complaints. Her cheeks were flushed, her eyes sparkling, and that damn maxi dress hinted at every curve of her ripe body without actually revealing anything.

It was driving me fucking batshit.

She lifted the pass, so she could enter into the big donut-shaped desk in the middle. Then she bent over the desk as far as she could, and I leaned toward her on my side of it. If I stretched just a little more, I could take her bottom lip between my teeth and—

"What's it called?" she asked.

"We haven't finalized it yet. The marketing guys are throwing a bunch of shit at the wall to see if it sticks, and they're running some focus groups. There's nothing that goes with the word 'toy' that really works, and—"

"Stella."

My jaw clicked shut and my hackles went up when she said my daughter's name. "What?"

"Stella means star. This place is shaped like a star."

I thought about it. Stared at her mouth moving. Tasted the air around her radiating enthusiasm. "Stella," I repeated.

Of course I'd thought about the munchkin when we envisioned this place, but more in what I thought she might like, or what I wanted her to check out someday. But I hadn't realized that I'd literally *built* her into the design.

My daughter hadn't seen it yet, even. The store was in the final stages of construction, and I wanted a woman's opinion on it—a woman who wasn't my heinous bitch of an ex or someone who already worked for the company.

The woman here in front of me—*this* woman—already knew more about me and what I envisioned for this store, than any of the woman who worked designing it for me.

"This woman" was also looking at me curiously, her forehead wrinkling. "I'm sorry, did I overstep or something? It's just my opin—"

I used my mouth to stop her apology.

My hands to grapple her instead of my own thoughts.

My arousal to match hers.

I kissed her deeply, like if I swallowed her it would take away the loneliness I sometimes felt. At the same time that I recognized my own need for Evie, I realized she was Dom's. Or was she?

All these thoughts ran through my head in a few seconds my tongue explored her mouth.

Evie moaned, her fingers flying over my shoulders and chest as if looking for a place to land. "Oh god, Jake. You're so…" She squeezed the thick, hard muscles of my biceps.

"You are, too," I assured her. "So…" I trailed off, not sure what either of us meant—only that we wanted each other.

Needed each other.

I leaned back, waiting to see if she'd follow. She did. My gasp sounded too loud in the empty store as she felt the ridges of my abdomen. When she pulled up my t-shirt to flatten her palm against my six-pack, her fingers resting in the dents between the corded muscles, I honestly thought my dick would explode.

"Evie, *fuck!*" I grabbed her hands and pulled them away, but didn't let her go. I held her there silently, looking down at the angel in front of me and hoping she was ready to fall from heaven.

Her head tilted back and she licked her lips as her expectant gaze met mine. It was such an unconsciously flirtatious gesture, not studied or fake. Some women were experts at that shit, and dumb enough to think it worked.

Then again, some men were dumb enough to fall for it. I wasn't.

"Jake, I want you," she stated, her cheeks reddening.

"I know."

"I want you to want me."

"I do." Our fingers, still twined together, curled into a large fist between us.

Evie bit her lower lip, making me groan. Goddamn, she had no idea what she was doing to me. And I felt more than a little *wrong* having a rock hard erection in a kids' toy store. Not taking her eyes off me, she untangled her hands from mine and pressed her palm over the bulge in my faded jeans.

Jesus fucking Christ.

"I want you to want me, *hard.*"

No more clarification was required. I needed to get her out of this store and into my bed, where I would fuck her as hard as she'd let me.

～

*W*ithin thirty minutes we walked through the front door to my apartment in the city. Like Dominic, I didn't want to live at the big house—trapped in all its trappings.

Our little virgin—no longer, I had to remind myself—nearly tore off my t-shirt as soon as we got our shoes off.

Lips, hands, tongues, fingertips—all over me, over her. We left a trail of clothes in the hallway, too impatient to get at each other to undress in the bedroom.

Fuck that, we didn't even make it to the bedroom.

"Jake, want me!"

"I *do*."

My spine tingled as her hot breath washed over my bare chest. I stood in the glow from the living room lamps, naked and unashamed in front of her. My weeping cock arched up between us, twitching as it searched for her warmth. Lazily, I circled the base of my dick with my fingers and stroked up and down. *Yesssss.*

Evie gazed at it, licked her lips again. Then, with a shimmy, she pulled her long dress over her head.

Pink underwear. Rosy pink, like the color of her hard nipples or her wet pussy. I sighed. Or I groaned. I wasn't certain, and it sure as fuck didn't matter.

Silently, she wrapped her fingers around my throbbing length, her knuckles bumping up against mine where they rested at the base.

We stood at least a foot away from each other. Her hand on my dick was our only connection. But somehow, I felt closer to Evie than I had to any woman in a long time. Maybe ever. It made me feel that weakness again—that strange sensation in the pit of my stomach that exposed a hole in my soul.

Enough of that shit.

I reached out to pull aside the soaked crotch of her panties. Tickled her entrance with my index finger. She was slick and hot, swollen and sensitive. I stroked, lightly at first, testing her by the sound of her shaky breaths.

Then plunged my first two fingers in.

And she fucking *loved* it.

"Ahhh!" Her grip on my cock loosened as her head tilted back in shock and pleasure.

"More?"

Her head wobbled from side to side in one last extinction burst of hesitation, until I added another finger.

"Shit! Yes!"

As the lady wishes. I dropped to my knees before her and yanked her panties down her supple legs. Evie screamed with delight when my tongue followed the path my fingers had taken.

She tasted like honey. I licked every part of her that I could reach from where I knelt, from her juicy cunt back to her back entrance, which clenched reflexively. Gently I rubbed my fingertip against the tight hole to assess her reaction.

Her reaction was to put her hands on each side of my head and squeeze like a vise as she pulled me closer. When I dipped my little finger inside her ass, just to the first knuckle, she let out a guttural moan.

"Oh my god," she panted. "That feels so—I can't explain it. It feels so naughty."

"It can be. More?"

I looked up to see her nod. My mouth and chin were

wet from her arousal, and I sought out her clit with my tongue. It wasn't hard to find—swollen and hard and sensitive, like her own secret little erection.

I dragged the flat of my tongue over it. Her hips jerked as I felt her walls clamp around the fingers that I still had in her pussy.

By now, my dick was having a temper tantrum at being ignored. And Evie's legs were getting wobbly, flailing out for the back of the couch in order to stay upright.

In my opinion, being upright was overrated.

Our breathing changed a little as I withdrew my fingers and tongue, and got to my feet. Forcefully but gently, I whirled her around and pushed her head forward.

"What—?"

My feet planted shoulder-width apart, I bent her forward over the back of the couch. Took a second to luxuriate in the feel of her soft ass against my belly. Then I bent my knees a little and impaled her on my cock.

"Ah! Oh my fucking god!"

"I'm wanting you," I ground out. "*Hard.*"

She squealed and shrieked as I drove into her tight, hot channel. For a moment I wondered if she was like this with Dom. Her skin was flushed and damp, our skin slapping together as I thrust again and again.

"Yes, Jake! Fuck me harder!"

Or maybe Dom got the Madonna, and I got the whore.

She wanted it hard? I'd give her hard. The fleshy top of her ass shook with every stroke. "Like this? You wanna be a little bad, huh?"

Every time I withdrew and entered her again, her

tender little cunt squeezed around me. She shrieked, but I was pretty sure it wasn't with pain.

I was balls deep in Evie, and it wasn't enough! I needed to face her, needed to bite her pillowy tits and watch the flush of her arousal spread over her neck and chest.

With a growl I pulled away, my hands around her waist.

"Jake, nooooo!"

"Don't whine." I turned her around and lowered us to the ground with more gusto than grace. My hands pushed her thighs apart roughly, then roamed over her breasts, hips, belly and shoulders while I knelt between her legs.

She reached for me, but couldn't quite get a grip on me. Her hands wrapped around my wrists to stroke up and down my muscled arms.

I bent over to take one of her nipples in my mouth, sucking hard enough to make her suck in a sharp breath. Then the other one. She exhaled with a hiss, wriggling her lush hips to get to my dick.

Re-entry was a little rough, and we both cried out. Within a few moments, though, we'd found our rhythm again. At first I slid my palms under her ass and pulled her to me. Then I leaned over her and braced my hands on either side of her head as I fucked her.

Hard.

I'd consider her rug burn a trophy of sorts, just like the way my knees were probably getting red and sore. But it was so worth it.

Again.

Harder.

"You're so tight, Evie."

"Love your cock. Fills me… so deep!" She couldn't even form a full sentence as she looked up at me with darkened eyes. Then they rolled back and her mouth stretched into a tight grimace.

"Oh god, I'm coming!"

"Look at me, Evie!" I demanded. In her spasms, she struggled to focus on me. I bent over to bite her lower lip, which got her attention through her soft pants. "Who's making you come? *Who?*"

"You are!"

"Not Dom, right?" Yeah, I might be a little competitive with my "brother," but show me a man who wasn't.

She shuddered as her climax ebbed, her voice softening. "It's you, Jake. You're making me come."

My eyes fluttered closed in satisfaction. *Yes.* I owned her. Even just for a few hours, she was mine.

She felt up and down my arms again, but her touch was shaky. My hips kept thrusting, jerking against her. Precum surely dripped from me now, painting her swollen channel, brushing against the entrance to her womb. My balls contracted and a rush of primal desire mixed with fear ran through my body.

Out of the corner of my eye, I saw a picture of Stella on a side table.

My baby.

Shit! I couldn't risk it. Evie might be mine right at this moment, but her future belonged to Dom—even if she didn't know it yet. I couldn't—wouldn't endanger that.

My balls began to tighten, and in one swift motion I pulled out and held my dick as my cum shot out onto her soft belly and thighs.

She sighed a little with each hot splash. In disappointment? Approval? Her eyelids were heavy and her smile mysterious as she watched me lose control all over the fucking place. I panted heavily, trying to get myself together.

"That was fucking intense," I said. She nodded.

"I'll say," I heard Dom say drily. "Would you like a damp cloth or something?"

My softening, wet dick smacked against my thigh as I pivoted around to see him standing by the front door. His arms were crossed and his eyes flashing.

He did not look satisfied.

EVIE

The irony is that I really did want a washcloth or something at that moment. It might have felt incredibly sexy to have Jake come all over me, but now I just felt exposed and sticky.

I sat up, bending my knees and wrapping my arms around my legs. Dom's dark gaze burned into me, but I refused to feel ashamed. Embarrassed, on the other hand…

"What the fuck is going on here?" he demanded. The low and even tone of his voice was more menacing than if he'd yelled.

Jake, who didn't seem at all interested in putting clothes back on, just tilted his head at his brother. "The 'fuck'—as you said."

I kicked him, my toes connected with his outer thigh as he sat back on his knees. He shot me a warning look, as if to silently say "This is between me and him."

The hell it was. When I glared my foot flailed out again, he grabbed it and circled my ankle with his long, talented fingers.

Dominic stepped further into the apartment. The closer he got to us, the more hurt I could see in his expression. It was the pain and jealousy that made my stomach twist now, not humiliation.

"Evie," he began, then stopped.

He looked up at the ceiling, his jaw clenching as he breathed deeply. Lowering his head, he glanced around until he spotted my dress. When he picked it up, his nostrils flared.

Without looking at me, he thrust the dress at me. "I need a minute with Jacob."

It wasn't a request. It was a dismissal.

My face was probably redder at that moment than when I'd been in the throes of my orgasm. I pulled the dress on over my head. Jake's hand slipped off my ankle as I stood up awkwardly, but he tugged on the hem of my dress to get my attention.

"Don't leave."

Seeing as his semen was gluing my dress to my skin, I didn't plan on it. "Can I take a shower?"

He nodded and jerked his head down the hall, presumably toward the bedroom and bathroom that we never made it to. I'd find it.

As I rounded the couch, Dom startled me by stalking forward to grab my wrist.

"I don't want you to leave either, Evie. Really, I don't. I want to talk to you, too."

I looked at my bare feet, not sure what to say. The first reflex I had was to apologize, but I sure as hell didn't want to—nor did I think I should have to. So I simply looked pointedly at his hand on my mine until he let go. Before heading down the hall, I grabbed my purse from where I dropped it by the door.

I'd never experienced that kind of whirlwind of lust before—the kind that had me tearing off all my clothes and begging to be taken. Even more amazing to me was the fact that Jake did it.

As I went into the master bathroom, I realized that I'd never be able to eavesdrop on their conversation with thirty feet and two doors between us. So I got into the shower, lost in my thoughts.

I wouldn't say that Dominic had "romanced" me and Jake hadn't, but Jake just wanted me for *me*. Sure, he'd benefit from the asinine will being addressed, but I never got the impression that he cared all that much. It was more Dom that was bothered by it.

Jake's lust was feral, unvarnished, and totally without expectations. Actually, sex with Jake was the kind of experience that I'd imagined—no, *hoped* to have after offering myself up to the highest bidder.

I shuddered a little under the warm water at the realization that I could just as easily have been drugged and trafficked.

What the fuck was I thinking?

This horrifying thought was looming in my brain as I wrapped a towel around me, and my purse started ringing.

"Hey, kiddo!"

"Hang on." I rubbed the side of my head with the towel, not wanting to get water on my phone. "Annie. I was just thinking about you." *And not in a good way.*

"So that's why my panties were burning!"

"Ha ha."

"Where are you?" Annie asked. "You've barely been home lately. I've been forced to drink alone, and you know that's never a good thing."

"Actually, it was that last bottle of wine with you that got me into this mess."

I rolled my eyes and plopped down on the bed. The *made* bed, with hospital corners. Since Jake didn't seem like the type of guy to have a daily maid, I guessed this was a leftover from his military training. Everything was so pristine that I worried about leaving an imprint of my damp butt on the covers.

Then I realized how ridiculous that was, considering that my "damp butt" had already been all over Jake's living room rug.

"Where are you? Oh god, are you in jail? Is this your one phone call?"

"Annie, *you* called *me*."

"Oh. Right." Her laugh was husky and a little uneven. Drinking alone *was* a bad thing.

"I'm at Jake's. Dom's here." I'd told her a little about the scenario—at least as much as was plausible outside a smutty book.

So, basically, she knew very, very, *very* little.

"Are you naked?"

Did the towel count? "More or less."

Gasp. "Are they naked?"

"More or less."

"You *whore!*" She sounded positively gleeful about it. "You have to tell me everything. I'm so lonely and horny that I'm thinking about dating this wine bottle when I'm done with it. If you know what I mean."

My mouth fell open. "Oh my god! Don't you dare!"

She sniggered, and I realized she was joking. At least, I hoped she was joking.

I explained—again, as much as I could without

sounding completely ridiculous. Seriously, saying this stuff out loud made my brain bleed. I skipped the whole "need a baby to fulfill the terms of an arcane will" thing.

"Whoa," Annie interrupted at the part where Dominic came into the apartment. "I've had too much wine for this conversation."

"I haven't had enough," I muttered. I was willing to bet money that Jake only had beer in his fridge, though.

"Let's cut to the good stuff. You wanna get with both of them?"

"Annie!"

"Sweetie, that shocked gasp sounded about as fake as my favorite purse. But you'd be amazed how many people don't notice that it says Pravda, not Prada. People see what they expect to see. I already Googled your guys, and they're fucking hot. And rich. So what the hell's stopping you?"

I didn't even know where to start. And I guess I thought it out loud, since her next bit of wise advice was to:

"Start by walking back out there and decide which one you want in the front and which one you want at the back. Here's a tip—whichever has the smaller cock goes in your ass."

"Annie!"

Her chuckle ended in a little hiccup. "Okay, that shocked gasp sounded real."

"This is crazy," I said, looking to the bedroom door. No sounds came from the hallway. Or the living room. If they'd beaten each other to death, it had been done with silent ninja skills.

"Yep. But as long as everyone is safe and knows the score, what's the problem?"

I chewed the inside of my mouth silently. The problem was that I wasn't sure of the rules of the game, much less the score. Was I a team player? I'd already begun to embrace this new sexual part of myself—how far did I want to explore?

The idea of being with both of them was, frankly, super fucking arousing. I was probably leaking on Jake's bed, just thinking about it. Squirming and pressing my thighs together, I whined wordlessly into the phone.

"Do it, do it, do it, do it, do it, *do it*!" Annie chanted.

I nearly dropped the phone when there was a knock at the door.

"Evie?" It was Dom.

Annie was on a roll—or at least her second bottle—in my ear. *"Doooooooo i—"*

I hung up on her. "Just a second," I called out automatically. "I'm not dressed."

The door swung open. "That doesn't bother me." He stood there, leaning against the doorjamb, his arms crossed over his chest. His suit jacket had disappeared, and his shirtsleeves were rolled up to his elbows.

"Yeah, apparently you don't have a problem invading people's privacy."

"I have a key."

I huffed, reminding myself that I was a new woman who could be secure, independent, and like sex without apologizing for it. Two months ago I was only vaguely independent, so it might take some getting used to. To prove to myself, and to Dominic, that I didn't care, I stood up and dropped the towel.

It was hard to pretend that his admiring gaze didn't affect me, though. That the possessive, carnal way his gaze devoured me didn't make me tingle. And want.

Want him. Want them. Want it all. I'd had a taste of pleasure and now I was thirsty for more.

Goosebumps spread over my skin, my nipples tightening and jutting out like raspberries that weren't quite ripe.

"My little virgin," Dom murmured.

I held my head high. Water trickled down my spine from my still wet hair. "Not anymore."

If anything, his expression grew hungrier. "Yes, still."

Shaking my head, I looked around for my dress. "Pretty sure my hymen is history, Dom."

"No. *Mine.*"

I stilled, looking at him. He absolutely, one hundred percent, without a doubt, meant it. The tension between us hovered in the air, like steam from the shower.

His? Did I want to be his? The certainty in his voice both rankled my newfound independence and made me want to fly into his arms. At that moment, I really could have used an interruption by Jake.

Taking a deep breath, I tried to focus on getting dressed—until I realized I'd have to put my dirty dress back on. Frowning, I threw it on the bed and looked around for… what, a magical clothes fairy?

Dominic stalked toward me, unbuttoning his shirt. "Here," he said, stripping it off and handing it to me.

It was tailor-made for him, of the finest cotton and came down nearly to my knees. Every time I inhaled, I breathed him in. His scent surrounded me, made me dizzy and aroused.

Maybe all this sex stuff is just pheromones, I thought. My fingers trembled a little as I did up the buttons.

"Thanks," I said shakily, putting all the wrong buttons in the wrong holes.

Ha! If that wasn't a metaphor for my current sex life, I didn't know what would be.

He pushed aside my hands to take over. His lean, hard chest was only inches away, and I itched to touch him.

"Never let it be said that I wouldn't give someone in need the shirt off my back."

It was more than that. It was like he'd removed his armor and wrapped it around me for protection.

My heart twisted in my chest. No matter how sophisticated I thought I was now—*snort!*—I didn't want to hurt him. He'd been nothing but generous to me.

"I'm sorry, Dom."

The shirt crushed in his fists, he drew me closer. "When I walked in and saw you two—" His eyes were dark, his jaw tight and his Adam's apple bobbing as he swallowed the rest of his words.

My own throat hurt when I swallowed. "I'm sure it didn't look good."

"No. It didn't. It looked fucking amazing."

I froze in aroused shock as he swiftly undid the shirt again. "What?"

"Fuck, Evie—" He broke off, his voice hoarse. "You're so goddamn beautiful. All those curves and that sweet skin. You're a goddess, like an ancient statue come to life."

My breath hitched as he ran his broad thumbs over my aching nipples. Arching toward him, the burning need built again in my core. I bit back a moan.

He was right, before. All he had to do was touch me, and I was his. He kissed me, just to prove that I'd melt.

And I did. I was on fire, but I didn't know how to ask for—

His lips moved to my ear, making me shiver. "Seeing you both there, naked? His—*him*—all over you? It was the sexiest thing I've ever seen."

Come again?

EVIE

I was still processing Dominic's words when he tilted my world further.

"You know, we've shared before—Jake and I. When we were young and horny."

"Now you're older," I managed.

"And hornier." His hands traveled down my sides and hips, reaching back to squeeze my ass. "Are you, Evie? Do you want to try it?"

Breathe. Breathe, dammit!

"I guess it's my turn to butt in, now." Jake walked into the room. All he wore was the boxer briefs he'd discarded earlier, outlining a mouthwatering bulge. "Nice shirt. It would look great on my floor."

I giggled at the corny pick-up line. Jake had managed to break the tension and ramp up the heat in the room, at the same time. I leaned back out of Dom's embrace a little, but he still held me around the waist. "Does that ever actually work?"

Jake grinned as he stopped next to us. "You tell me."

He reached out and traced an invisible line up the back of my thigh.

A bolt of lust speared through my core. *Yes, yes it did work.* I took a few steps back, slipping out of Dom's grasp, and peeled the shirt off. Dropped it.

The armor was off.

Dom exhaled harshly. "Are you sure, Evie?"

I looked him in the eye, then Jake. Back to Dom. "I'm sure."

The truth was that the moment I'd met them, part of me knew we would arrive at this point. My body knew it, seeking out both men. My soul knew it, having connected on different levels with them.

I wanted this.

We were all silent, our heavy breathing the only sound in the room.

"Uh, what do we do now?" I asked. *There goes my sophistication.*

Dom brought my hand to his mouth. "Whatever you want, love." He pressed a kiss into my palm.

"I want… I want…" I took a deep breath. "I want both of you. In me. Filling me." Speaking the words made me feel brave and sexy—and unbelievably turned on. If I didn't keep my legs together, my juices would be running down my legs.

Then again, I thought, *if I'd kept my legs together, I would never be in this situation.*

Jake smoothed his hand over the expanse of my bare back, all the way down to the curve of my butt. "We'll get there. Right now, I want to watch you and Dom."

"Huh?" *Naked man say what?*

He jumped on to the bed and scooted backwards to

lean against a black leather headboard. The golden skin covering his muscles rippled and beckoned in the lamplight, and I could see the golden hairs on his arms gleam as he reached down and pulled his thickening cock out of his briefs.

Oh god.

"I want to watch him kiss you, and wish it was me. I want him to touch you while you look into my eyes, Evie."

Jesus. "You know this is a little weird, right?" My body reflexively squeezed in reaction, though.

"Baby, it's been weird since the day we met." I turned to see Dom's shoulders shake as he tried not to laugh at me. He didn't try very hard.

Well, that was true. I pivoted back to Jake. "Is this, uh, something you guys are, um, into?"

Jake chuckled. "Not really. We just both appreciate beauty, right Dom?"

"Beautiful," Dominic said as he embraced me from the back. While I was staring at Jake, Dom had shed the rest of his clothes. Now his hard-on pressed up against my ass and lower back, a promise and a warning of what was to come.

The only barrier between all of us now was Jake's boxer briefs and my nerves, and at least one of those was about to be discarded.

I swallowed hard, but the arousal overwhelming my body was winning over any prudish hesitation I had.

Dom's arms snaked around my middle, one hand going up to palm my breast, and the other diving into the cleft between my legs. It was a good thing he was supporting me, since my bones melted as soon as he circled my clit.

"Oooohhh." My head lolled back against his shoulder and my eyes drifted closed as he teased me. He rubbed, swiped, and plucked, raising every nerve ending until I was moaning loudly.

"Fuck, that's hot," I heard Jake say.

I opened my eyes to see him, now completely nude and looking like a risqué magazine spread, crawling to the end of the bed where Dom held me.

Dom offered his fingers to Jake, for him to lick clean of my juices. My lungs felt tight, like I was close to hyperventilating from sheer anticipation.

Dom nuzzled my neck from behind and moved both his hands to my breasts. While his thumbs teased my nipples, he nudged me forward, his erection hot and weeping at my back. We were now close enough to the bed that Jake could clasp his hands around my ass cheeks and pull my core to his mouth. I grabbed his shoulders so I wouldn't lose my balance and fall.

To be honest, though—I had already fallen.

I braced myself, knowing I was still a little sensitive from earlier, but he tongued me gently, tenderly. Dom's fingers on my nipples were rougher than Jake's lips nibbling my clit. In fact, he carefully worked around the most delicate spot, which both relieved and infuriated me.

"I need your—agh!"

"Way ahead of you, honey." Jake grinned up at me, his chin shiny from the arousal flowing from me. Then he zeroed in on the center of my pleasure until he and Dom were literally holding me upright.

"Oh fuck, I can't… *ah!*"

I felt trapped in my orgasm like a fly in a spider web. My thighs were splayed out, and I was balanced between Jacob's hands cradling my ass and his mouth at my pussy, and Dominic's palms around my chest and the tense column of his body. I couldn't even draw my legs together, so I jerked and throbbed helplessly.

When I could draw a deep breath once again, I realized that Jake and Dom had shifted all of us to the bed. Jake disappeared briefly, and when he returned with a few cold bottles of water, Dom was smoothing his hands over me like he was memorizing the lines of my body.

He paid extra attention to my belly, my hips and navel. I'd always wanted the flat, even concave stomach shown off by celebrities and even school friends. But I had stretch marks and flab that would only disappear if it were literally carved off. Inside I wanted to cringe as Dom kissed the extra padding on my hips and squeezed my flesh reverentially.

For the first time, though, I felt more feminine because of my curves—as though my body was made for this. I was made for loving, built for pleasure, and primed to grow a baby inside me.

Instead of being ashamed of my body, I suddenly felt as though I'd discovered its true purpose. It was a flash of lightning to my psyche and my identity.

I propped myself up on my elbows and looked down at Dom's head hovering over my mound. Balancing myself, I reached out and grabbed his hand where it rested at the bottom of my ribcage.

"Evie, what is it?" His dark eyebrows drew together in a concerned frown.

I laced my fingers through his and spread our joined hands out over my lower belly. "Nothing," I said. My voice was a little shaky, but my smile wasn't. "Nothing's wrong."

His thumb rubbed against my skin, and the heat of our palms sank through to my womb. "You are so amazing," he said.

"You make me feel that way." I pressed his hand harder against me. "I want you to put a baby in me, Dom."

His eyes flashed with gratitude, awe, and something else. "Don't do it for me, Evie. Or for the money. I know that's what I proposed, but I can't let you—"

"I'm not. *I want it*. God knows why, but I do. I'm twenty-two years old and have barely done anything, but I know that I want to be a mother."

Perhaps that was my calling in life, but I'd been too afraid to admit it. I was supposed to have a powerful career and make money and connections and prove I was as good as a man at everything. The truth was that I was far superior to a man in one elemental way—creating and nurturing life.

"Oh, Evie." Dom raised our hands over my head and lowered himself onto me. He kissed me deeply, his tongue sweeping away my fears and leaving certainty and self-awareness behind. His cock was hot and heavy against my thigh, seeking the wet warmth of my pussy.

Jake cleared his throat from where he stood beside the bed. "This is really touching and all, but are we still going to fuck?" He reached into the bedside table drawer for some lube and a couple of condoms.

Dom rested his forehead against mine and growled under his breath.

I giggled. "He's *your* brother," I whispered.

"Do you…?"

"I do."

His eyes widened at my words, as did mine. The

spell was broken when Dom rolled us over so that I was straddling him.

"I just need to be inside you," he grunted as he pulled me over his long, hard cock. I gasped as he penetrated me. Without pause he drove up into me until he was totally buried in me and I felt replete and full.

"Yes," he hissed. With his hands on my hips, he began shifting me back and forth, but I didn't need his guidance. I moved over him in an age-old rhythm, gasping again as his pubic bone rubbed against my swollen clit.

Jake ran his knuckles up and down my spine as I shimmied on top of Dom, making me shudder. I twisted around a bit to look back at him, giving him a nod.

"Lean over more," he instructed.

I flattened myself against Dom, my chest rubbing against his. The crisp hairs on his chest tickled my nipples, and my chin bumped into his sternum as I looked into his eyes.

"I can see where you're joined," Jake noted, making his meaning clear by tickling us both where Dom's cock impaled me. All three of us inhaled sharply.

I'd stopped moving on Dom, simply lying on him. He remained buried deep inside me, his arms around my back and fingers skimming over my shoulder blades. Instinctively I tilted my hips back toward Jake's touch.

"You have the most luscious ass," Jake murmured. His fingers, slick with lube, circled my rear opening, dipping in to press against my clenching hole once, twice, then enough times for me to beg him for more.

"Jake! *Please!*"

I held my breath as he carefully wiggled his whole

index finger into my ass, then moved it around in small circles to stretch and open me. With Dom still in my pussy, the dual sensations felt incredible.

"Okay?" Jake asked.

I nodded. When I tried to look back at him, the twisting motion of my torso made everything below tighter and more intense. "Oh!"

"Careful, okay man?" Dom warned Jake.

Jake slowly added another finger.

"Holy shit," I breathed out, my back stiffening.

Then Jake curled his fingertips inside me, rubbing gently against the flesh barrier behind which Dom was lodged. Pinpricks of pleasure zapped me, like tiny electrical shocks.

"Can you feel that?" Jake asked, but I wasn't sure if he was talking to me or to his brother. I didn't realize I was holding my breath until it whooshed out of me and my stomach relaxed against Dom's pelvis.

Jake barely moved his fingers, but the strange intensity of it made me arch my back. I asked for more, but maybe this was too much?

"Oh Christ, Evie." Dom reached up to palm my breasts, squeezing them. "I'm gonna come." His warning sounded like an apology as his chin tilted up and all the tendons and muscles in his neck tensed. He cursed as I felt him swell further inside me, then warmth flooded me.

At the same time, Jake withdrew his fingers, and the competing sensations rocked me into a guttural mini-climax of my own.

I collapsed onto Dom's chest, my body still pulsating. I turned my head to the side, my hot cheek resting against Dom's damp pec. Out of the corner of my eye, I saw Jake drop a foil-wrapped square beside us. He ripped another one open and rolled it on his own erection.

"Hey, you don't get to have all the fun, you know."

EVIE

*J*ake's hand smacked my ass playfully, making me flinch. Dom was still hard inside me, even after coming—either having recovered or never truly finished. I was too innocent still to know the difference.

Although, "innocent" probably wasn't the best way to describe myself after tonight.

I'd barely recovered my equilibrium when—actually, scratch that. I was nowhere near recovering my equilibrium after… whatever that was.

Already dizzy and breathless, it didn't take much to unseat me as Dom rolled us to the side. His cock fell out of me, sticky and half-erect between us. Swiftly he reached for the condom.

"Help me," he said. I wasn't sure what he meant, but I wrapped my hand around him, stroking up and down until he was impossibly hard again. "Yes. Fucking love your hand on me, Evie." He helped me roll the condom down, biting back a groan.

Then, to my surprise, he rolled me to my other side, away from him.

Jake was there, waiting for me, his own erection wrapped and sticking up to his belly. He shifted closer, running his hand over my thigh before pulling it up and around his hip.

"I should have used something before," he apologized gruffly. "Shit, I'm sorry. I wasn't thinking."

The realization that I hadn't thought of it either bothered me. "It's okay."

Being this close to him again sharpened my arousal, if it had ever dulled. His bulk and strength made me feel delicate and protected, his muscles hypnotizing me as they flexed under his skin. Lying side by side on the bed, we were almost at eye level. I couldn't look away.

"Open up, Evie." The command was teasing in tone and utterly serious in intent.

With one devastating movement, Jake impaled me. He swallowed my gasp with his mouth, his hips jerking softly against mine. At this angle, we were more in tune with each other, our motions slow and deliberate—to start. He broke our kiss to grin over my shoulder.

Before I could look back to see what Dom was doing, I *felt* what he was doing.

"Oh!"

"'S'okay, baby. Just relax." His slick finger circled my rear entrance, sliding down now and then to tease both Jake and me where we connected.

Jake rolled me further over him, hitching my leg higher to give Dom better access. My heart thumped in my throat as he paused inside me.

Dom's breath was hot on my neck as he curved around my back. His broad hands cupped my ass, spreading me open and tormenting me with tendrils of intense pleasure. I was on high alert, all my senses acutely aware of what was happening.

"Breathe." Jake reminded me, blowing a playful breath against my parted lips.

My head tipped back a little. I looked at the leather headboard while trying to open up my throat and lungs.

My heart and soul were already split wide open.

Gently, slowly, I felt Dom broach the ring of muscle behind where Jake still filled me. Instinctively, I held my breath and stiffened up in anticipation. It was so tight! He nudged further in, stretching me until I winced. There was no way he was going to fit in *there*.

"You gotta *breathe*, honey."

"Oh *god*!" When I let the air out of my lungs, Dom's well-lubed cock passed the narrowest point, sliding into me fully.

"Fucking hell, Evie." He panted into my hair, his voice husky. "You took me all the way in your ass, baby."

Jake shifted his hips, reminding me of his cock still lodged in my pussy. Like I could forget?

I was so *full*. I didn't know I could feel this replete. They surrounded me, lay siege to me, invaded me. But I felt… complete at the same time. Secure, sheltered, loved. These men were my armor now—my defense against the rest of the world.

"I have to move," Dom ground out.

Twisting my neck as far as I could, I met his anxious gaze and smiled at him with encouragement. "You know you can't get me pregnant this way."

"You got me. This is just fun." His grin was tight around the edges as he struggled to stay still. "I don't want to overwhelm you."

Too late for that. I laughed, and both men groaned.

If I thought the sensations of both of them embedded within me were intense, it was nothing to what I felt when they found a rhythm sawing in and out of me.

It was indescribable—the density, the fullness, the keen knowledge that we were all together.

Dom's mouth clamped down on my neck while Jake ran his tongue around my lips again. Their arms wrapped around me, their hands steadying, pushing and pulling at the same time.

My fingers curled, digging into Jake's muscular back and then reaching back to find Dom's flank. Pulling them closer to the edge with me. Their grunts and hoarse curses echoed in my ears. Every inch felt like a foot; every second lasted a minute.

All the while, the pressure building in me had nowhere to go, except for streaming through the rest of my body. Even with what little experience I had, I knew that this orgasm would be like nothing I'd felt before.

"I'm close." Jake's upper lip was damp with sweat, his chest rubbing against mine. "Dom?"

"Fuck, yeah. But Evie…"

I didn't know if they were referring to me, or speaking to me directly. Clumsily, roughly, hands—I didn't know whose—snuck between us to find my throbbing clit.

Within a few seconds, I felt both of them swell within me, hot and hard like freshly blown glass.

And I burst.

I think I screamed out that I was coming—at least it felt like it. But my voice was hoarse and small, all the room inside me taken up by pleasure. For a split second

I wished they weren't wearing condoms, so I could feel the hot flood of their release.

We were all damp with sweat, hot and trembling as we slowed to a stop. It probably wasn't possible, but I thought I could hear their heartbeats as well as mine, thundering in my ears. Urgent grasps softened to feathery caresses and a low hum of satisfaction vibrated between us.

Wow. Holy fuck.

Jake kissed me and closed his eyes as he withdrew from me. Instantly I felt the loss. Dom enclosed me in his arms, his voice low in my ear.

"Okay, Evie?"

"Mmmm."

Carefully he pulled out, and for a moment I felt discomfort as my body resisted, then like a deflating balloon he was gone.

I scissored my legs back together and rolled onto my back. The ceiling blurred above me. Jake and Dom disappeared for a moment into the bathroom then returned with a damp hand towel.

"Is that warm or cold?" I asked, telling my body to lift an arm. It didn't.

"Does it matter?"

"I guess not."

I lay there quietly as they kneeled beside me on the bed and took turns sponging me down. Wiping my sweat away, soothing any aches and pains.

If I closed my eyes, I could almost imagine that I was in a spa. Okay, a pretty fucking *adult* spa, but it was still relaxing.

When I licked my lips they tasted salty. Jake handed me a half-empty bottle of water, still a little cool from the fridge. It felt amazing filling my mouth and going down my throat. The weight of their gazes on me was almost as heavy as their bodies.

What were they expecting me to do? To say? To feel? I let out a heavy, contented sigh.

"Well, that happened."

DOMINIC

Sometimes it was easy to forget how young Evie was.

Inexperienced in so many ways, she had a knack for altering my perspective on things I thought I already knew inside out. She had an old soul, but then there were reminders of her age.

Like her first question after our threesome: "What's the rule for this stuff and social media? Instagram? Change my Facebook status to *it's complicated*?"

Jake laughed so hard he nearly fell off the bed. Evie's beautiful, flushed face twisted into a frown when I chuckled, as well.

"Insta—! Gram—!" came a wheeze from the floor.

I kicked Jake from where I sat on the edge of the bed. "Be a gentleman, you jackass!" Then I hissed at him under my breath, "How is she supposed to know?"

When I turned back to Evie, mentally preparing a lesson on sexual etiquette for social media—about which I knew very little—the mischievous curve of her lips stopped me. She was playing us?

My blood boiled. There was only one logical course of action—tickling.

"Oh noooooo! No, stop!" Her hair flopped into her face as she writhed on the bed under my relentless fingers.

I found some particularly sensitive spots just under her ribs and behind her knees. This was almost as much fun as—well, *almost.*

"Stop laughing," I teased her, making my voice forceful and stern. "This is not funny, not at all. This is —" I let her gulp and catch her breath, then walked my fingertips up her spine. "Serious! Business!"

If anything, she laughed harder. And I was having a pretty hard time keeping my composure, too.

"Dominic! No m-more!" Her face was red and tears leaked out of the corners of her eyes. "I'm sorry, I'm sorry! I'll never tease you again!"

My touch went from tickling to tender. I raised my hands and brushed the dampness off her face with my knuckles.

"Well, that would be a damn shame," I said.

As she settled down and sighed, her gaze locked to mine, I realized that Jake was in the shower. It was just the two of us.

"Are you sure you're okay?" I asked her.

She raised her arms over her head and stretched like a centerfold. "I'm fabulous."

Her nipples were still rosy from our attentions, and love bites marked her creamy skin like a constellation. Just when I thought she couldn't get more gorgeous, she upped the ante by wearing my passion on her body.

"Yes, you are." *Smack!* Her playful slap was as inconsequential as a mosquito bite. "Seriously, though." I raised my eyebrows, giving her the opening to tell me the truth.

"I'm fine, Dom. But…"

Shit. What had we done wrong? I leaned over her, bracing my hands on either side of her. "But what? Tell me."

Fuck, had I hurt her? Been too possessive? Not possessive enough? My heart raced as I waited for her reply.

She clasped her hands together and lowered them over my head, her arms circling my neck. "You were right about tickling being a serious matter. Especially naked tickling."

This girl was killing me. "Evie! Jesus!"

She tugged my head down, close to her face, until the tips of our noses brushed against each other. "Dominic Stone, I am fine. That was a.." She had to search for the right word. "Extraordinary experience, and you—and Jake—made it that way. Thank you for loving me like that."

My eyes widened and I jerked my head back. Evie's eyes nearly bugged out of her head, before she snapped them shut and covered her face with her hands.

"Shit, I'm so sorry. I shouldn't have said that. I don't know what I was saying. I meant 'love' in the physical sense of copulation. You know, a biblical kind of knowing. Or in English literature, like when they say they 'made love' it's just really flirting or kissing behind a fan in a rose garden or something—"

I covered her runaway mouth with my hand. She opened her eyes as I snaked my other arm under the small of her back and pulled her upright.

"You done?" I asked her.

Under my palm, I felt her bite her lip. She nodded. I

lowered my hand, and kissed her swollen lower lip. The shower stopped in the other room. Silence curled around us like steam escaping underneath the door.

"Thank you for letting me love you like that," I finally said.

I knew what I was saying. I knew what words I was using, and what they meant. Not the classic literature version or the 'begats'—though that wouldn't be a problem—but she had bewitched me. It sounded stupid, but I couldn't find a better word to describe her effect on me.

This whole thing had started because she needed money, and I needed to fulfill the idiotic terms of Grandad's will. But Evie had shown me her own will of steel, and suddenly all the money in the world didn't matter to me as much as she did.

It was official—I was a fucking sap.

"Marry me," I blurted out.

Her lips parted—because, somehow, a proposal was more shocking than a proposition. "Because I might be pregnant?"

Something primal thrilled inside me at the idea that she could already be pregnant, but I shook my head. "No, because I want more."

Her laugh was high-pitched and nervous. "How much *more* can I give you?" She rolled her eyes, not meeting my gaze.

It was still very quiet in the room, and I suspected that Jake was eavesdropping on the other side of the bathroom door. God knows I would be, in his place.

"You. I want *you*, Evie."

She closed her eyes, muttering to herself. "This is so nucking futs. I must be out of my mind."

"I *know* I'm crazy. But let's be crazy together."

"What about Jake?"

The bathroom door opened. "What about Jake?" he said, a towel wrapped around his waist.

Evie's eyes flew open and fastened on my brother. Jealousy curled in my stomach at the way she looked at him, but then I realized that she looked at me the same way.

"I don't want to make you feel bad or anything—" she began, until he held up his hand to stop her.

"Evie, I knew from the beginning you were for Dom. I just wanted *him* to know that." He grinned. "Don't get me wrong, it was fun. But I've got too much shit on my plate to try being in a relationship."

"Stella," she murmured. He nodded.

Relief filled me. "So, Jake's not an issue. What about you, then, Evie? Do you want to live with me? Want to see this idiot at family dinners? Have our baby, travel the world, live in luxury?"

Her gaze swiveled from Jake to me. "I can't have this conversation while I'm naked."

Jake unwound the towel from his body and threw it to her on the bed. Now he was bare-assed for this conversation, but he didn't care. In fact, he disappeared back into the bathroom and shut the door.

Leaving us alone again.

"I need time to think about this," Evie told me. "I'm not going to marry you just because I'm desperate."

Her desperation was what brought us together. I didn't see anything wrong with it. Though, I was going to have to come up with a better story for Grandad and his lawyers. It would really help things along if I'd knocked her up.

As though she could read my mind, she asked, "What about your grandfather?"

"Fuck him."

She made a face. "Ew. I don't think I can give you *that* much more."

"Seriously, I don't think I care anymore. My shares in the company are worth enough that we could start over. I'm tired of being under his thumb."

She jumped up from the bed, clutching the damp towel around her. "Then why the hell didn't you do that in the first place?"

I blinked, my mind blank. *Holy shit.* For someone who ran a giant corporation that revolved around figuring out what people wanted, I was pretty fucking dumb. Maybe she would be better off with Jake after all, but I wasn't going to let that happen.

Evie grabbed my rumpled shirt off the floor and hastily buttoned it up. "I need to go. I need to think."

I followed, grabbing her. "Don't go when you're angry."

She stared at my hand on her arm, and I dropped it. "I'm not angry, Dom. I'm just... confused. I have to figure out what I really want. I never expected to be in this position."

I looked back at the bed, the sheets still smelling like sex. For that matter, I was still naked.

"*That* position, too," she added, her lips quirking. She reached up to kiss me. "Don't worry." She zipped away, pausing to grab her shoes and purse before slamming the front door behind her.

Sighing, I ran my hand through my hair. "Easier said than done."

It felt like she was running away—from me, from

security, from the potential for a lifetime of happiness. The irony was that I was the one who gave her the financial freedom to escape. All she had to trade was an inconsequential piece of flesh.

Somehow I'd handed over my heart for her hymen.

It wasn't a fair deal.

"Well," Jake yelled from behind the bathroom door, "you sure fucked that one up!"

EVIE

When I'd said I needed time, I didn't mean three weeks. But somehow I'd entered an alternate dimension, and life had gotten in the way. I also spent way too much time talking to Annie about Dom's proposal.

"You're gonna have to get a better lock on your door, Evie. Damn, you're lucky I don't rob you, myself!"

Annie picked up a magnum of very, very expensive champagne and looked at me mournfully. It was only one of the dozen or so extravagant gifts that Dominic had sent me. It was like the freaking Twelve Days of Christmas—only in autumn and thankfully with a lot fewer birds.

I knew he was waiting for an answer. I also knew that patience was not Dominic Stone's strong suit. The last few gifts had been a top of the line smartphone, a new laptop, and—most bizarrely—a framed antique bookplate of a passenger pigeon.

He was trying to communicate something…

"Just do it," Annie urged.

I gaped at her. "You're seriously encouraging me to marry someone I've only known for a couple of months?"

"People have gotten hitched in Vegas after knowing someone for a couple of hours—most of them shit-faced," she pointed out. "Do it, do it, dooooo it!"

I flopped onto the bed in the corner in a new silk nightgown—compliments of He Who Must Not Be Tamed. "The last time you said that, I ended up in bed with both of them."

"Poor baby," she scoffed, rolling her eyes. "Don't make me cry."

I rubbed the charmeuse fabric of my nightie between my fingers and stared at the ceiling.

"You forget," she added, "I've seen both of them now, in person. You'd have been a fucking idiot to *not* go for it."

Three days before, I'd found Jake and Annie chatting outside the front of the building. Jake had his daughter in a jogging stroller, and his old dog tags stuck out against the sweat-soaked t-shirt he was running in.

I looked down the street, half-expecting to see a trail of panties that had been dropped by female passers-by. The only thing that would have made him more… ovary-exploding would be if he had a puppy with him.

At first, I wasn't sure if I should even talk to him, but as far as I knew he had no hidden agendas. He showed me pictures of the sign that was being designed for *Stella*, and didn't mention Dom's name once.

After some polite chitchat, he handed over a box that was stashed in the bottom basket of the stroller and picked up the pace back down the street, winking over his shoulder at us.

Annie and I *might* have watched him until he reached the end of the block. As we headed inside, I was shocked to find my smart-ass friend beet red and almost silent. Apparently Jake was Kryptonite for her sassy mouth. He was closer to her age than mine, actually, so I thought they'd get along better. Maybe I was wrong.

Maybe I was really, really *right*.

"What was in that box, anyhow?" Annie asked from the couch, having put the champagne back on the table.

"I haven't opened it yet." It sat on my bedside table, a red satin ribbon tied around it.

I sat up on the bed to rest against the cool wall. The slim spaghetti straps of the ankle-length nightgown extended down my back almost to my butt, leaving my entire back bare. Despite the stretchy lace cups and underwire top holding me in—which felt a little too snug and scratchy on my boobs—I was a little worried that the slinky gown would fall off if I leaned over.

It was beautiful, and what's more—it made me *feel* beautiful.

Dom had been very good at making me feel beautiful. The prospect of having that for the rest of my life was a little terrifying.

We both stared at the little white box.

"Is it ticking?" she joked.

I shook my head. This was the last gift to have arrived, and then nothing for the past few days. Something inside me knew that this was the most important one—the big sell, maybe. It was probably expensive. It might be rare and amazing. It could be irresistible.

That's what I was afraid of.

Annie cleared her throat. "C'mon, Pandora. Open the box." My eyes widened in surprise, until my friend blushed. "Just because I'm a waitress doesn't mean I don't know my Greek mythology."

"You know she let out plague and pestilence, right? All the world's evils."

"Don't forget about hope." She tilted her head as I carefully put the box on my silken lap. "Do it, do it, do it, dooooo it!"

Hope was something in short supply in my life for the past few years, until I met Dominic and Jacob Stone. The irony now was that I was afraid to hope for it. The two men had changed my life, changed *me*.

What would my life be, now?

The ribbon was as smooth as my nightgown between my fingers, the knot slipping open and trailing over my thighs. The box was too small to be a car, and too big to be an engagement ring. Then again, packaging could be deceptive.

The top flaps fit together like a flower's petals, and I opened up the bloom to peer inside.

"Oh my god."

"What is it? Is it a head? Did he send you a severed head?" Annie squinted at the box. "A shrunken head?"

I shook my head and pulled out a mangy, stuffed toy dog. Tied around its neck was a dented, scratched silver object—a rattle, maybe?

The way my heart rattled in my chest told me that this was more important than any piece of jewelry, any rare flowers or techie toy he could give me. Instinctively, I knew that this was part of Dom's childhood—a part not normally shared.

A scrawled note tucked into the box confirmed it.

Grandad got this dog for me the day of my parents' funeral. I remember using its paws to wipe the tears off my face. I was eight. The silver rattle was the first gift that Grandad gave me, according to family lore. They were the two most important things in my life, until I met you. I hope someday we can give them to our children, if we're that blessed. When you open this box, come to me. If nothing else, I need to know that you got it.

I got it.

I'd give anything to have my parents back again, even if it meant staggering under the weight of massive debt. But I'd been lucky enough to have most of my life with my parents. Dominic hadn't enjoyed that luxury.

"You're crying," Annie pointed out from where she lay on the couch. "It *is* a head."

I laughed, sort of. It wasn't until I automatically raised the stuffed toy to my face that I realized I, too, wanted to use it to dry my tears. I sniffled, my stomach curdling at the discovery that all this time, Dom wanted a family as much as I did.

He wanted to belong to someone, to *me*.

I'd only been considering how much I needed him, and worried about taking advantage of him. It hadn't occurred to me until that moment that perhaps he needed me more.

The silk of my nightgown made it easy to slide off the bed. "I need to see him."

Annie sat up, frowning. "Now? It's eleven o'clock at night!"

I stopped, one flip-flop on and the other dangling from my big toe. The dog was held to my chest, tucked between my breasts by my left hand.

"Really?" It was that late?

She nodded.

"Then what the hell are you doing here?"

"Uh…" Annie was at a loss for words, almost as much as when she met…

"Jake!" I shouted. Jake would know where Dom was. *Probably. Maybe. God, I hoped so.*

"What?" Annie fell off the couch with a bump. "Shit, where?" Her head turned from side to side so fast it looked freakily demonic.

Ignoring her, I grabbed the phone out of the charging dock and sent a text to Jake's number. Within seconds I got a response.

Where else? The office.

"Annie, I gotta go." I shoved the other shoe on my foot. "Get out of here so I can lock up." *Phone, shoes, purse…*

"Evie, you can't go out like that."

I looked down at the floor-length silk negligee. My tender nipples were pointing through the lace cups.

"You're right." I put the bear, the rattle, and my purse in a tote bag, and pulled on a college hoodie.

∼

*I*f the night guard on shift at the Stone building's security desk thought my outfit was strange, he didn't let on. He was all business, to a fault.

"Miss, the elevators are locked for the night. Only people with keys can access them. I shouldn't even have let you in the front doors, but you looked… cold."

I hugged my tote bag to my chest. "You have a key, don't you? I just need to see Mister Stone. I know he's here. I even know where his office is. You don't even have to get off the elevator with me—"

He held up a hand. Sighed. "How about I call him to come down to see you?"

"That would be great." I sagged in relief—literally, the hem of my gown brushed the polished floor. "I'm sure he'll want to see me."

The guard looked me up and down, raising an eyebrow. "Yeah, I'm sure he will."

I would have been offended, had I not looked like a psycho sorority girl.

While I waited, I moved to the giant coat hanger sculpture I'd noticed on my first visit. Under halogen lights, it looked much different—more like a glistening spider web.

What kind of patience would an artist have to have to balance and solder together a thousand hangers like that? What did it mean—that there was beauty in consumerism? Or was it like the retail version of the Emperor's New Clothes? You couldn't help but admire it; but at the same time, there was nothing there.

I heard the click of footsteps on the floor behind me. Hugging myself, I tried to regulate my breathing and kept my eyes on the sculpture.

"What do you think?" Dom's voice was low and husky in my ear.

"It's stronger than I first thought." When I first saw the piece, it had looked to me as though it could collapse any moment. Now, I saw it and realized that every element was carefully balanced to support another.

"You opened Toby."

That must have been the name of the toy dog. "I brought him with me," I said, swinging the tote bag.

"He was special to you, so he's special to me. Thank you for sharing him with me."

Dom still stood behind me. "There was nobody else I've ever wanted to introduce him to. Not even Jake knows about him."

Oh.

"Evie…"

He stepped closer to my back, the heat from his body penetrating the thin silk around my legs. His hands skimmed over my shoulders, the tips of his fingers trailing through my hair.

"What the hell are you wearing?" he growled.

I spun around, needing to see him. "My past," I said, grabbing the zipper of the hoodie. Then I tugged the zipper down to expose my chest. "My future?"

It was difficult to look in his eyes when his gaze was riveted to my cleavage. In my flip-flops, I was nearly a foot shorter than him, as well.

"You're going to have be more specific than that, sweetheart."

This was turning out to be both harder and easier than I'd thought it would be. "You know how the ad said that I wanted to be loved?"

"Yes," he said slowly.

"I didn't write that—Annie did."

"Ah." His lips pressed together tightly.

"But that doesn't mean it's not true."

"Ah." His lips parted. "There's something I forgot to mention in our previous negotiations." I tilted my head back as he put his arms around my waist to pull me against him.

"Another amendment?"

"I love you, Evie. I know it sounds crazy, and maybe

it is. I don't have a lot of experience with love. I'm practically a virgin." He chuckled. "But when I asked you to marry me, it wasn't out of pity or some kind of twisted benevolence."

"I know. I love you too."

"It was because I—wait, what?" His hands tightened around my waist, the heat of his palms searing me through the thin silk.

"I. Love. You." I slid my hands over his chest, dipping into the gaps between the buttons of his shirt. My senses gloried in the feeling of his skin under my fingertips.

His relief was palpable. "Damn right, you do."

He bent his head to kiss me hungrily, molding his body to mine until there was no space between us. When I was good and breathless, he raised his head an inch. "You'll marry me," he announced.

"I'll marry you."

"You'll put up with Jake."

"Eh." I shrugged. "It's not that hard."

"I'll fight my grandfather for you."

"You don't have to. I'm already pregnant."

His head reared back in shock, his mouth curving with delight. "Really?"

I blushed. "I think so. I haven't taken a test yet, though. But I feel pretty weird, and I don't think it's the flu." I clutched at his shirt. "Will you still want me if I'm *not* pregnant?"

"Baby, I wanted you as soon as I met you. In case you hadn't noticed, you drive me fucking crazy with desire."

"I didn't know I could feel that way," I whispered.

All of it—the dates, the intimacy, the friendship, the sexual adventures—they were all a revelation.

He rested his forehead against mine. "Neither did I. My little virgin turned into quite the vixen."

I raised an eyebrow. "Rawr." My sexy growl made us both laugh. "You know, I never got that coffee and muffin from our first meeting."

"Right," he recalled. "The virginity bonus. You can have all the pastries and coffee you want—decaf, though."

"I like it with two sugars and lots of cream."

"Done. Shall we go up to my office to get you that, uh, sugar and cream?" His eyes darkened with need, and this close I could feel his body tighten against mine.

This time, when I swayed toward him, I definitely couldn't blame my flip-flops. "Your office is fine."

"Excellent."

And they lived happily ever after.

**Except for Jake.
Now it's his turn.**

~

Keep reading to find out how Jake and Evie's friend Annie find their happy ending! Hint: it involves ninjas and negligées.

A HARD PLACE

ANNIE

I didn't become truly uncomfortable until he slipped something into my box.

Something twisted in my chest, like a vague kind of panic and I literally bit my lip in order to stay quiet.

I'd been receiving anonymous notes at the restaurant for a month already. Sure, customers had left their phone numbers on the table before, but these came in envelopes, typed and printed. Nothing threatening, just random quotes from love poems.

A week ago, one of the notes came with flowers. The large bouquet of roses was signed, "Your secret admirer." Then a box of very expensive chocolates showed up two days ago.

It was all completely unoriginal—and totally unnerving.

That kind of thing might be cute when you're sixteen, but I was closing in on thirty this year. What's sweet and thrilling as a teenager is considered stalking when you're an adult. Instead of my heart going pitter-pat, my fingers went tap-tap as I called the police.

Their advice was to be more aware of my surroundings, keep the notes and throw away the gifts. Oh, and to bring the evidence down to the station if my admirer began delivering cookies—especially if they were chocolate chip.

Thank god there's no city ordinance against eye rolling, because I broke the bylaw when I heard that stellar suggestion from law enforcement. I knew they weren't trying to make fun of me, but I still felt kind of helpless.

I *hated* feeling helpless. I'd spent my "sweet and thrilling" teenage years taking care of my single mother as she bounced from spineless boyfriend to loser boyfriend, to asshole boyfriend—one or two of which I'd had to junk punch.

I knew how to kick ass and take names.

I'd *had* to learn.

Now, I hesitated outside the door to my building as I watched the tall, broad back of the man in *my* lobby, at *my* mailbox. Even from a distance, I could tell he was a lot bigger than me. Surrounded by the darkness of the night, I felt vulnerable and exposed.

Should I call the police? Should I yell for help? I gritted my teeth, not liking either of those options.

I ducked back outside the halo of the security light just before he came out the door. I looked away, as if it would make me invisible. When I turned back, he'd begun jogging down the sidewalk in the opposite direction.

I followed.

Adrenaline and stupidity surged through my body. The aching fatigue in my body from a long-ass shift disappeared, leaving only the strength in my legs and arms from years of waitressing.

My slight frame in my cushioned slip-on shoes barely made any noise as I crept behind him. My uniform of plain black pants and a button down black shirt kept me in the shadows—or so I hoped.

And I still followed.

The closer I got, the more I realized that my stalker had a fucking incredible ass. I'd only seen rear ends that spectacular a few times in my life. His jeans hugged his lean hips and hung on his legs like rock star groupies.

The muscles in his back and shoulders shifted under his thin black t-shirt, and even in the darkness I could see the tan on his arms. His hair was cut close to his head—so close I wasn't sure what color it was.

Okay, so my stalker was hot. I could admit that. My heart was going pitter-pat now, but that was probably from the exercise. I stubbed my toe on the pavement in my effort to be stealthy, and caught a curse before it fell out of my mouth.

He slowed his pace, his head cocking to the side. I froze, even holding my breath. Of course, if he turned around he would see me standing a dozen feet behind him. In the glow of the streetlights.

Well, hell—I was a waitress, not a ninja.

Then my phone rang.

I nearly jumped out of my skin. A hushed *"Motherfu—"* burst out of my chest before I could stop it.

Somehow I managed to dive behind a mailbox at the same time as scrabbling through my cross-body purse to mute my phone.

Yes, I multitasked the *shit* out of that situation.

I glanced down and declined my best friend Evie's call, hoping she wouldn't call back again. Flicking the switch to "vibrate," I peeked out from behind the mailbox.

Stalker Sweet Cheeks had paused on the sidewalk about twenty feet away, his body stiff. His head whipped from side to side. From my angle, I could see his jaw clench slightly and muscles flex in his forearms. I pulled my head back, waiting to see if he'd keep walking.

Passing cars managed to hide the sounds of my feet shuffling in my graceful squat behind the mailbox. When a car slowed down in front of me I smiled at the driver, but he didn't look reassured that a woman crouching behind a USPS box in the dark was totally normal.

I startled, nearly falling on my ass, as Sweet Cheeks stepped off the curb not far from me. My heart stopped, then started again as he bounded across the street in between cars. He disappeared into a dive bar on the corner without looking back. Then I slumped against my metal hiding spot.

What the fuck was I doing? Was I completely loco? I was stalking my stalker.

My phone buzzed in my hand, Evie's face lighting up the darkness.

"Hello."

"Hey, Annie! Where the heck have you been? I've been trying to get a hold of you!"

"Working. A lot," I lied in a low voice.

Evie paused for a moment. "Where are you? You sound weird."

My sore legs protested as I straightened. "I'm just, uh, getting home from work."

I kept my head down, close to the mailbox. It smelled like what pennies tasted like.

"Now you sound like you're in a tunnel or something," Evie said, then she gasped. "Oh god, are you in trouble? You need to tell me if you need help but can't say it. Say something like, uh, I had to stay late to fill the ketchup bottles."

I'd told Evie about my mystery man, and she'd been more concerned than I was at the time. In fact, she'd been the one dragging me to the police station to file a useless report.

Honestly, I think they only pretended to listen to her because I told her to bring cookies. Afterwards, I told her that they'd probably be more impressed that she was engaged to Dominic Stone, billionaire retail magnate.

Money talked. Cookies walked.

"I'm fine," I said. "But I'm following *him*."

"*What?*"

I held the phone away from my ear as she shrieked.

"What do you mean, 'following him'? Stalker dude? Where is he now? Where are you?"

"He just went into a bar." My gaze flicked up to check on the door at the corner again. "I came home and found him stuffing something into my mailbox, Evie."

"What was it?"

"Dunno. I decided to tail him instead."

"You're nuts. He could be dangerous, Annie. You should go home and put gloves on or something before opening your mailbox. Then take whatever it is to the police."

"What if there's a severed head in there or something?"

She snorted. "The mailman can't even get a book from Amazon in those dinky boxes. I hardly think it's going to be a head."

I hummed. It could still be a head. Maybe an animal's head?

The idea made me shudder, and the hairs on the back of my neck stood up. I felt a sudden urge to take my long dark hair out of my ponytail, like having it falling around my face would protect me somehow. It was a silly idea, but I did it anyway.

"Wait!" Evie's voice startled me. "Did he *open* the box?"

My eyes closed with the memory. "No," I said slowly. "It looked like he was putting something through the cracks, like an envelope."

"So it's probably just another creepy love poem."

"Just another" was one more than I wanted. I was about to point that out to her, when I saw his back halfway down the block on the other side of the street.

Damn it! I'd missed him coming out the door.

"Shit! He's on the move," I hissed into the phone, popping out from behind the mailbox and trying to catch up before I lost him.

"Did you get a picture of him?" Evie asked.

Duh. I did a mental face palm. "Gotta go, call you later." I hung up on her and switched my phone to record video.

It was hard to keep up—but not too close—and stay focused on him, especially from across the street. It would probably look like a shaky horror movie from a film student. I'd be lucky if he was even in any of the shots, frankly.

I was so focused on keeping his large, muscular body

in the frame, that I didn't notice that we'd done a big circle and were approaching my apartment building again.

No way.

Stalker Sweet Cheeks leaned against the waist high concrete wall bordering the steps up to the front door, and pulled out his phone. His neck flexed as he bent over it.

Any fear I'd had was replaced by anger. Was he going to wait for me here? Follow *me*? Ambush me? Kidnap me?

This was *my* fucking apartment! My home, my sanctuary. My wine storage facility.

I put my phone back in my purse and swung it to my back. Darting through the dark, I rounded the building and went in the back door that people use for moving furniture in.

Sure, I could have just snuck up to my apartment and left Sweet Cheeks out there twisting in the breeze for however long he decided to stay. But then I'd be afraid every time I went out the door.

Not again.

The time for being helpless was over.

My mental rundown of what I was taught in self-defense class was brief. All I could remember was to get the higher ground and go for the eyes. I spread my fingers around my keychain, but my electronic front door fob and single apartment key weren't much of a weapon. I didn't even have a car fob to try to club him with.

When I looked through the wall of glass at the front door I saw him at the bottom of the steps, still engrossed in his phone. My gaze swung up and down the street.

The traffic was still pretty regular, but the sidewalks were empty.

I waited until a big truck was rumbling by, then snuck out as quietly as I could, wedging my purse in the jamb so I could escape quickly behind the locked door if I needed to. The solid concrete railing was wide enough for me to jump up on, and edge my way down the dozen steps to where he stood.

"Aaaaaaaahhhhh!"

I jumped on his back, clasping my hands around his throat.

My legs wrapped around his waist, and while my whole body was taut with adrenaline, his was just *taut*. It was like clinging to the concrete wall itself—only warmer. And smelling… amazing?

"What the fu—?" he growled, whipping his head around. His skull connected with my nose, bringing tears to my eyes.

Goddamn, that hurt!

His growl turned to a grunt as I tightened my fists, jabbing my door fob into his windpipe.

Swiftly, he pivoted away from the wall. My legs lost their hold, flailing as he dropped into a squat. Then his hands wrapped around my wrists so hard I swear I felt the bones scrunch together.

"Owwww!"

My grip loosened as I yowled in his ear. With a sharp exhale, he held on to my forearms and flipped me over his head to the sidewalk.

At that point, I was willing to concede that maybe jumping him was a bad idea.

The wind was knocked out of me, my wrists burned, and my back stung like a sonofabitch. I was lucky my head hadn't hit the ground, but the sharp pain in my neck told me that trying to avoid a concussion was going to end up in another injury. At least my arms weren't broken.

I catalogued all these things in about three seconds, while I lay there breathless. Blinking.

Then he dropped on top of me, one of his knees bending to pin down my thighs, and his hot, hard forearm across my throat. His breath was hot on my face, and smelled a little like bourbon.

"Why are you follow—*Annie*?"

He jerked back up, his hands going to his head. I sucked in a breath, my ribs aching. For the first time, I saw his face clearly in the security light at the front door.

"Jake?"

My stalker was my best friend's fiancé's brother?

JAKE

"Holy shit!"

Evie's friend Annie lay before me on the sidewalk, gasping for breath.

I'd put her there.

What the fuck was she doing, jumping on my back like a deranged monkey?

She stared up at me, her big brown eyes wide and her face pale. Her long dark hair puddled around her head like blood.

Holy. Shit.

"Are you okay?" I knelt beside her again, my gaze skimming her body to check her over. No blood.

"Fine?"

She didn't sound fine. She was making the same kind of choked, rasping noises that my daughter Stella did when she had a bad cold.

I had to admit that she looked fine, though. *Really fine*. Annie was a tight little package of hotness, like a shot of good espresso. I frowned.

"Why are you dressed like a ninja?"

"It's… my… work… uniform… dumbass." With each word she was able to take a deeper breath, until the color began to return to her face.

"You work as a ninja? I hate to say it, but you had some shitty training."

"You're hilarious." She rolled her eyes and winced as she pushed herself up on her elbows.

"Hang on." As I wrapped my hands around her arms to help her up to a sitting position, she yelped.

Right. I'd grabbed her there—hard. Self-loathing curdled in my belly. I never thought I'd hurt a woman like that.

Sure, there were times that I wanted to shake some sense into my ex—and baby mama—but I'd never laid a heavy hand on a chick before.

Unless she wanted me to.

I reached behind Annie, curling my arms around her waist and upper back, and pulled her toward me. I kept my arms around her once she was in a seated position—just in case.

She smelled faintly of food, the scent of coffee in her hair. But as she slumped against me, I smelled the faded remains of the perfume she must have put on that morning. It was spicy and exotic—a little like her.

My jeans tightened as my body reacted to the woman in my arms. Then my brain reacted.

"What the hell were you thinking, jumping on me like that?" I'd gone from turned on to pissed off. "I could have seriously hurt you!"

Her forehead creased as she scowled at me. "What the were *you* doing, messing with my mailbox?" Her sharp nod toward the door of the apartment building was accompanied by a little moan at the movement.

"You saw me? Why didn't you say something?" I released her, leaning back on my knees to see if she'd remain upright without assistance.

She did. In fact, her spine looked like it had rebar running through it.

"I didn't see *you*, Jake. I saw a *guy*. A tall, hulking stranger with his fingers in my box."

I couldn't help it. My mind went to a dirty, dirty place at her words. The smirk on my lips widened.

"What's so funny, asshole? You're the one tampering with the mail, which—I might add—is a federal offense!" Her words came faster than her movements as she rose to her feet. "How would you like to come home from a hard day at work to find a strange man shoving something in your slit?"

Laughter burst from me. It was impossible to stop it.

She stood in front of me, her hands on her hips and an indignant expression on her face. On my knees, my line of sight was squarely on the general area of her "slit." And I chuckled again.

"Honey, I sure hope you *don't* have strange men fingering your slit." I hopped to my feet.

She spluttered, her cheeks reddening as she got the joke. "That's not what I meant."

"That's what I heard."

"Pervert."

I raised an eyebrow at her, remembering her ogling me the one time we'd met before. I'd been running with Stella in the stroller, and stopped by to drop something off for Evie. The admiration in Annie's eyes had followed me all the way home—and into a long, hot, handsy shower.

Even though that had been eight months ago, my

cock still hardened at the memory, threatening to embarrass me. And it took a *lot* to embarrass me.

I bent over her, so close I could smell her perfume again. "I've been called worse."

When she tilted her head back to look me straight in the eye, hers were dark and glittering. "I bet," she said faintly.

I had to give it to her, though. She didn't drop her gaze. Okay, she dropped it a little, but only as far as my chest. I felt it like a physical touch, a shiver of arousal shooting up my spine.

Throwing her to the ground didn't even make me break a sweat, but being this close to her took my breath away.

Stepping back, I scrubbed my hand over my head.

Annie blinked once, twice, like she was waking up. "So what were you doing with my… mail?"

"Wedding invitation."

Her mouth fell open. "You're getting married?"

"Hell, no!" I recoiled. "Evie and Dom are."

"Oh, right." She looked down at the sidewalk, her fingers fiddling with her scuffed purse. I hadn't noticed it before, but she was damn lucky I hadn't accidentally strangled her with the damn thing. Irritation flared in me again at her stupid ninja moves.

I sighed. "Apparently you haven't RSVPed or something, and Evie's been calling you? She asked me to hand deliver it, to make sure you'd gotten it, but you weren't home…" I hadn't realized how late she worked. Then again, I wasn't even sure what she did for a living. I asked her.

"I waitress."

"Not a ninja, then."

She cracked a smile, which somehow made me feel fucking proud. "No, not a ninja." Her eyes narrowed as she added, "I talked to Evie earlier. She didn't say anything about you dropping it off."

"Well…" I rubbed the back of my neck. "I was supposed to do it a week ago. Maybe two."

"Two weeks?"

"Three at the most."

"Shit," she muttered. "Has it been that long since I talked to her?" she asked herself out loud.

"I guess she thinks you're avoiding her."

Her gaze flicked to me. She twisted the strap of her purse nervously. Guilt was written all over her face.

Oh.

"It's not that I'm *avoiding* her; I'm just—"

"Busy?" Yeah, I'd heard that one before. I'd even used it in the last couple of weeks.

Annie exhaled. "I hate weddings." Judging by the look on her face, she equated weddings with something like leprosy, or bars on Saint Patrick's Day.

"I thought all girls loved weddings. Pretty dresses, catching the bouquet, hot groomsmen…" Again, my mind travelled to a naughty destination.

"Expensive, ugly dresses you only wear once, being humiliated in public for being single, and obnoxious assholes thinking you're so desperate to get married yourself that you must be an easy lay." She ticked them off on her fingers.

"Hmmm. Well, at this wedding, I'll be one of those obnoxious assholes."

My imagination began working on a mental picture of her in a silky dress. Would she even wear a bra? Her breasts were a perfect handful, but then maybe the material of the dress would rub against her bare nipples and make them stand out…

"I'm not desperate."

I blinked as she spun away and began walking up the steps—slowly. "Hey, hey, let me help you."

"Thanks, Jake. I think I got enough help from you, already." Her voice was flat and fatigued.

I followed her into the building, standing at her back as she opened her little mailbox. Inside was a slightly bent envelope with her name in calligraphy on it. She jumped as I leaned against the vault of mailboxes.

"I didn't know your last name was Asato, by the way."

"Asshole," she muttered under her breath.

"What? Did I pronounce it wrong?"

"No. You didn't."

I ignored her eye roll. "What kind of name is that?"

"Japanese. And before you ask—no, I don't speak the language and I've never been there. My father died when I was a baby. And I fucking *hate* sushi."

I flinched, as though the bitter acidity in her tone might have pockmarked my skin. *Someone had issues.*

"What kind of name is Stone?" she mocked.

"It comes from Old Icelandic, and means a bubbling river or stream."

Annie Asato inhaled sharply and frowned at me with confusion.

"I'm just fucking with you." I stood up straight, flashing her a wide smile.

The relief on her face was obvious, but she slammed her mailbox shut with a metallic clang and turned her back on me.

Note to self: Annie did not like being made fun of.

The one and only time I'd met Annie, I'd been trying to disengage my heart and hormones from the brief and blazing liaison I'd had with Evie, her best friend.

I wasn't blind, though.

Any man would have brought her to mind when alone in the shower, with her long dark hair that begged for a fist to wrap around it and tug it back. Her tight little body, and her sassy, sarcastic tongue.

In some ways she was the polar opposite of Evie's bouncy blonde hair and ripe curves. Evie was like overdosing on marshmallow treats, resulting in a sugar high then regretting it later.

Annie, I suspected, would be like sucking on high quality dark chocolate. The taste would linger.

That was a good thing—and at the moment, that good thing was walking away from me, to her low-rent apartment in her low-rise building.

"Hey, wait!" She didn't pause in her trudge up the stairs. Her ass bobbed hypnotically in front of my face. If I reached out, I could just... I shook my head. *What was I...? Oh, right.* "You got a date to the wedding?"

She halted, then gasped when my body collided with hers. I could have moved away. I should have moved away.

I didn't.

I repeated the question.

"No, of course I don't have a date!" she snipped as she spun around on the step above me. "I was hoping I could avoid going altogether."

"No need to be petulant, princess. From what I hear, you're the maid of honor. You kind of have to show up."

"Ugh. Fine! I'll be there." The pained expression on her face told me she'd rather have a root canal.

"So go with me. I'm the best man."

Her expression was incredulous.

Unable to deny my curiosity any longer, I reached out and ran my thumb and forefinger down her long, silky hair. Now her expression was inscrutable, but her eyes widened.

"Why should I?" she asked me quietly.

Damn, I'd never had to work this hard to get a date. "Because I'll make it fun for you. I'll protect you from the assholes, and I'm a fan-fucking-tastic dancer."

"I can take care of myself."

"I'm sure you can. You're kind of a ballbuster." I held up a hand as her delicate eyebrows drew together and her lips parted. "In the best kind of way."

"Ha!" She rolled her eyes. "I haven't seen a scrotum in two years, much less busted one."

Could have fooled me. But now I was even more intrigued by this exotic ninja waitress.

"So? The wedding?"

She poked me in the chest. "You know I'm not fucking you in the coat room, right? I refuse to be a cliché."

My easy grin belied the tightness in my groin. "Too bad. I'd let you bust my balls."

ANNIE

At first I thought the big box that appeared at my apartment door a week later was from Jacob Stone. After all, it held a slinky gown, high heels, and luxurious lingerie. Maybe he'd hand-delivered my bridesmaid's dress. Actually, it wasn't as awful as I worried it would be.

Then I saw the note.

"Roses are red. Violets are blue. I think this would look sexy on you." –Your secret admirer

Oh my god.

He had been just outside my door. Had it been locked? I sometimes forgot to lock the door when I was home. I must have been home when he delivered it, since it wasn't there when I got home from work. I'd been sent home early when the whole downtown block was notified of a gas leak.

I found the box when I headed downstairs to check the mail after a shower and an afternoon nap. When I realized that working near open flames during a gas leak might be safer than my own apartment, I got scared. Then I got angry.

Then I got out the wine.

Three glasses later, my fear had not dissipated. My knee bounced nervously as I sat on a scarred wooden chair at my kitchen table. Wondering what to do. The box mocked me from across the room, where it sat by the front door. It was too bad that it wasn't from Jake, because everything in it was something I would have chosen myself.

That was the most frightening part. This person *knew* me. A random creeper was easier to ignore, somehow. I looked around my tiny studio apartment with new eyes.

Maybe the bamboo blinds on my windows didn't give me enough privacy. Maybe I shouldn't have let the building maintenance guy come in to fix the leaking trap under my sink. Maybe the previous tenant had left secret cameras installed in the light fixtures. Maybe the guy who'd moved into Evie's old apartment next door had drilled a hole through the wall and was spying on me.

Maybe I was being a little paranoid.

My anxiety drove me out the door, nonetheless. If I wasn't safe in my own home… Walking outside, I felt even more conspicuous. Was my secret admirer watching me? Following me?

Sure, I could run in the sneakers I wore and my baggy sweatshirt and tight leggings wouldn't get in the way, but I was still a petite woman—who had already demonstrated her pathetic ninja skills on Jake the previous week.

Jake.

Now, Jake could hold his own. He could hold me, too.

The dog tags that swung from his neck the first time I'd met him told me that he'd served, so he surely knew how to fight—if the way he'd flung me over his head wasn't a reminder.

And if I remembered correctly, he'd had a baby in the stroller that day. He was probably a very protective father to the little girl with blonde curls and an obstinate look. She was freaking adorable. So was the fact that Jake had named his new toy store after her, or so Evie had told me.

Evie had also told me that she'd hooked up with Jake, and had a wicked threesome with him *and* Dominic. At the time, I'd hooted and egged her on. I mean, they were both super hot and super available— why the hell not?

Now, however, I felt uncomfortable allowing myself the fantasy of Jake's big, hard body sheltering mine. His strong arms could shield me from harm—or they could lift me up while he fucked me against the thin wall of my apartment. I could lean on his ridiculously broad shoulders, or I could feel them under my thighs as he tasted me. I suppressed a small shiver at the mental image.

Was it even appropriate for me to think about him, when he'd seen my best friend naked?

Then again, I'd seen Evie naked before, too. Plus, I'd loaned her my underwear. Nothing says BFF like sharing ass floss—which she could keep forever, as far as I was concerned.

She'd assured me, through blushes and stammers, that the three-way was a one-time thing only. It had been a wild, hedonistic moment that had never repeated itself—nor did she really want it to. She was committed to Dominic Stone, and soon she'd be tied to him for better or for worse.

The sidewalks were filling up with people heading home after work. Was I safer in a crowd, or was my stalker just more easily camouflaged?

I didn't want to go home. He could be waiting for me there. Or at my favorite coffee shop. Or at the gym. Okay, probably not the gym—since I hadn't been there in months.

There was only one place I could think of where I would be safe.

I hopped in a cab to Evie and Dom's castle in the sky. The penthouse downtown was where they spent most of their time, and I hoped Evie's standing invitation still stood. The welcoming delight in her voice when I called up from the security desk was an arrow of guilt in my chest.

"You've been avoiding me!" was the first thing she said when I exited the elevator directly into the apartment.

I tilted my head just in time to avoid a nasty collision as she yanked me into her arms.

"Oof!"

Evie's warmth and softness made my throat hurt. Had it been that long since I actually hugged somebody?

My friend stepped back, wrinkling her nose. "You've been drinking."

Holding up my thumb and forefinger, I said, "Just a little. Stress management."

"I do yoga for that, now."

"Good for you."

"And have lots of sex." She stuck her tongue out at me.

"*Great* for you."

I wasn't jealous, I wasn't jealous, I wasn't jealous.

Evie's sunny mood lightened mine by sheer proximity. The wine hadn't made me giggle, but now I felt the urge. It was just so damn good to see Evie happy.

A miscarriage the previous fall had dimmed her spirits, but Dom really came through for her with every kind of support he could provide. Now it was spring, and Evie had… sprung back.

Like I said, I wasn't jealous.

She led me into the kitchen, where I hopped onto a stool at the granite-topped island the size of a lifeboat.

"Grilled cheese?"

I pressed my fist to my heart. "Does this mean you forgive me for not being a great friend lately?"

"Not totally," she said as she dug out a pan. "I'm giving you only one kind of cheese."

I wasn't about to complain. Experience reminded me that she made them the right way, with buttered bread and sharp cheddar sliced off the block.

By the time we ate our sandwiches—one of which she delivered to Dom where he was hunkered down in his home office—I'd finished telling her about my secret admirer and my stealth attack on Jake.

"You're staying here tonight." It was a statement, not a question.

I nodded.

Evie's assertiveness had definitely grown in the last year. You might even say she'd become a bit bossy, but it was a relief to have someone else take care of me—even if just for a few nights.

The bedroom she put me in was cozy and the pajamas roomy. Much to my surprise, I was out as soon as my head hit the pillow. If they had kids already, I'd suspect that she sprayed the pillowcase with Monster Be Gone or something like that.

I hadn't realized how badly I needed a solid night's sleep, but I was still groggy when I headed to the kitchen in search of coffee. The long hem of the borrowed pants nearly tripped me as I rounded the corner and found Evie completely without her pajamas. On the kitchen island.

"Fuck me harder!" she cried out.

She wasn't talking to me.

"Oh my god!" I spun around and clapped my hands over my eyes. Then my ears. Shit, why didn't I have four hands? "I'm sorry, I'm so sorry, I didn't—*agh!*"

Evie's muffled, breathy voice filtered between my fingers. "Did you need something?"

"Coffee." And maybe brain bleach. Or a vibrator.

Even more embarrassing than interrupting such an intimate, carnal scene was the way my own body had immediately reacted. My skin tingled, and heat stabbed through my middle.

"Do you still want coffee?" Dom sounded more amused than angry.

I took my hands off my ears and put them over my eyes again as I instinctively turned back toward the kitchen. "Yes. *No!* Fuck, no!"

"Yeah… that's not something I hear often." He snickered.

"Apparently." *Go. I needed to… go.* "I'll just go out or something."

"Is that safe, Annie?" Evie asked.

"Is what safe?"

I never understood the saying "she jumped out of her skin" until Jake's voice echoed in my ear.

"Agh!" He stood so close behind me that I nearly head-butted him in the chest when I spun around in shock. My hands went to his hard chest, ready to shove. "What the—?"

"Morning, Annie." He grinned down at me and wrapped his hands around mine, holding them to his hard chest. Then he nodded casually over my head at his brother and his... what? Ex? Soon-to-be sister-in-law? "Hey, guys."

There was no embarrassment in his discovery of the couple's intimacy, no hesitation in his acceptance of it. The jealousy burning in my chest irritated me, as did his sneaking up on me.

I tugged my hands away and crossed my arms over my chest, forgetting that I might still need eye and ear protection. "Where did you come from?"

Jake shrugged. "I know the elevator code. And *I* went to a *good* ninja school."

My face warmed at the memory of jumping on his back. It grew hotter as I imagined jumping on his front. "Uh..."

"Wow," he murmured, "that's quite a blush." I froze in shock as his palm cupped my cheek. His gaze swept over my face and down my neck and chest. "What *are* you thinking about?"

It was a good thing that my hands were still tucked under my armpits, because they were probably shaking.

Every time I saw Jake, my composure was exponentially disturbed. The first time, I ogled him. The second time, I attacked him. The third time, I went up in flames as he simply touched my face. What would happen at our next encounter? Would I survive it?

Did I want to?

"I'll make you some coffee," Evie announced, interrupting my quickly derailing train of thought.

"Baby, noooo," Dom whined.

I heard a quiet grunt and the sound of bare skin skidding across polished stone—probably Evie's backside as she tried to get off the island.

"No!" I began to turn back to the kitchen, but Jake's hands went to my shoulders to still me.

"Do you really want to do that?"

He had a point. His palms smoothed up and down my upper arms in a soothing motion. I bristled a little at being treated like an agitated animal, but remained still and facing him.

"I mean—it's okay. I'll go down the street or something." It was a big city. There had to be a Starbucks on every other corner. "I'm sure it'll be fine, Evie."

Jake's gentle caresses stopped, his grip tightening just above my elbows. "*What* will be fine?"

"Annie has a stalker."

"Evie!" I closed my eyes, embarrassed. I'd been taking care of myself for a long time. Certainly I could deal with a garden-variety creeper, right?

"What do you mean, a stalker?" Jake's voice lowered and roughened with each word, until he was practically growling.

"You know—notes, gifts, showing up at her apartment," my friend explained helpfully.

One of Jake's hands went to my chin, tilting it up. My eyes flew open; his searching gaze pinned me to the spot. "Is that why you flipped out on me last week? You thought I was…"

"Maybe. Kind of. Could be." I tried to look down, but his hand held my face up. The best I could do to escape was close my eyes again.

It seemed unlikely that I would ever mistake Jake for a stranger again. His body—hell, his mere *presence* imprinted itself on me with every meeting. I'd never had this kind of reaction to a man before. It was like my frayed nerves were reaching out to him, twining and fusing together.

I hated feeling vulnerable like this. It reminded me of the times I'd longed to be comforted as a child. Now Jacob Stone was evoking all these feelings in me again—feelings that I'd spent a long time trampling down underneath me.

He rubbed my jaw with his thumb. "And that's why you're wearing Evie's pajamas? You stayed here last night?"

"It's not a big deal." I shrugged, looking at the floor. Not wanting to know how he knew they were Evie's PJs. Then again, they didn't seem like Dominic's style.

"Why didn't you tell me?" he demanded.

Was I supposed to? My chin went up again. "It didn't concern you."

It really didn't. I'd been taking care of myself for a long time. It never occurred to me to tell him about my secret admirer. It was embarrassing enough to have one.

His hands dropped from my face, making me suck in a quiet breath.

I felt the absence of his touch more keenly than when he first he laid his hands on me. My skin felt exposed, like I'd been too long on the beach without sunscreen.

"Didn't. Concern me," he echoed. His voice was as flat, dry and hard as the Arizona desert—without the heat.

"As fascinating as this all is," Dominic said, "I'd like to get back to fucking my fiancée. You stay, you play."

My eyes widened as Jake's lips curved up. *Oh god.*

"No, I'm taking Annie for coffee."

And he grabbed my wrist and pulled me toward the elevator.

JAKE

*M*y fingers completely circled her wrist. *How easy would it be for a psycho stalker to grab her?* I wondered.

"Jake!"

I ignored her protests until I heard her bare feet slap on the tile floor in the foyer. "Put your shoes on."

Her voice echoed behind me. "Um, what about—"

"*Shoes*, Annie. Put. Them. On."

I slapped the button to call the elevator harder than necessary then scrubbed my hand over my face. Like I didn't have enough on my mind? Now I was imagining some asshole sniffing Annie's hair while she slept.

Motherfucker.

"But—"

I sighed. "No buts. Unless you want to take your clothes off and join those two in the kitchen, we are leaving. I'll get you your fucking coffee, and you can explain why having a stalker doesn't 'concern' me."

It wasn't until we were in the elevator and almost to the lobby when I really looked at her. Her expression was a mixture of irritation and anxiety, and the pajamas made her look like she was twelve.

Pajamas. *Shit*.

Well, I didn't really care, to be totally honest. Nonetheless, I steered her to the closest coffee shop at the end of the block, so her walk of shame would be shorter.

"This is so embarrassing," she muttered as I shoved her down onto a chair.

"Sit."

She popped back up like a spring, glaring at me. "I'm not a dog, Jake."

I shook my head as I went to the counter. *Damn contrary woman.*

"You didn't even ask me what I like," Annie grumbled when I got back to the table with drinks and a couple of muffins. At least she was sitting down now, and she hadn't left. She turned the side of the cup to peer at the shorthand order written on it.

"I got you a mocha with an extra shot of espresso."

She pouted. "What if I didn't like chocolate?"

I blinked at her, speechless. Didn't all girls like chocolate? Shit, even Stella loved hot cocoa when it was cold outside.

Annie said nothing more as she delicately sipped the drink. Satisfied that she seemed to be able to choke it down, I tore off a piece of muffin and shoved it in my mouth.

She was playing me. *Again*.

Her slim fingers wrapped around the paper cup as she took bigger and longer sips. With each passing moment she seemed more energized, yet calmer at the same time.

She was so intent on her coffee that she didn't even

notice a couple of women staring at her, probably wondering why she was wearing PJs. I stared them down until they lowered their gazes and moved on to a table on the other side.

We sat in silence until we were half done our coffees, and the frown lines on her forehead had vanished.

I sat back in my chair, crossing my arms over my chest. "Okay, tell me everything I don't know."

Her eyebrow lifted. So did the corners of her mouth. "We could be here a while."

What? Oh. "Smartass."

The grin she flashed at me was completely disarming. I suspected that Annie Asato had a wicked sense of humor when not being targeted by some lovesick creeper. That information just made me feel... wicked.

Her cheeks turned red as she haltingly told me about the notes—which she brushed off—and the gifts. When she admitted that he'd left sexy lingerie right outside her front door, I sat up straight with two competing thoughts: How the hell did he get into the building? And how hot would she look like in the lingerie?

"Jake?"

I shook my head. "What color was it?"

"The box?"

"The panties."

She reached for her coffee. "Seriously?"

Now it was my turn for a disarming grin. "Just kidding!" *Sort of.*

"Sure, and *I'm* the smartass." She snorted and rolled her eyes as she tilted her head back to finish her drink.

Annie had a very long neck, I noticed. Other than a faint crease, probably from looking down at her phone, it was unblemished and very, very...biteable. Her shoulders probably were, too. It wouldn't take much work to undo a few buttons of the oversized pajamas and slip the shirt off to expose them. As my gaze wandered over her, I realized that she wasn't wearing a bra.

I was attracted to her, sure. But the way this woman turned me around was starting to irritate me.

It wasn't that I disrespected women. It had just been my experience that they were either goodhearted but naïve—like Evie—or lying whores. Maybe that was harsh, but Stella's mom sure hadn't endeared me to the gender as a whole.

Annie didn't fit either of those descriptions. She was tiny but tough, wary but reckless. It was pretty dumb of her to jump me when she thought I was her stalker— even dumber and more dangerous if I actually *had* been the dude.

"I can put you up." The words came out of my mouth before I registered what I was saying.

"Uh, escoof me?" There was still muffin in her mouth when her lips parted.

"Let's face it. You can't take care of yourself."

"Can't…" She swallowed. Her face turned a kind of purple color, and her eyes were bugging out.

Shit. "Are you choking?" I asked her, enunciating carefully and mentally reminding myself how to do the Heimlich. "Put your hands to your throat if you're choking."

"Can't take care of myself?" she spluttered.

Oh. "No offense, honey. But we already know how shitty your ninja moves are. I'd feel better if you stayed at my place—which I *know* is safe—while we figure out who this asshole is and how to get rid of him."

She blinked. "There are so many things wrong with that statement, that I don't even know where to start."

"Can you fight off a man who's got a hundred pounds on you?"

Silence.

"Can this guy get into your building?"

More silence. There was a mulish set to Annie's chin, reminding me of Stella when she didn't want to get out of the bathtub.

I sat back, sighing. "Are you looking for trouble?" My muscles tensed as she kicked the leg of my chair.

"*Mumble mumble* coffee with you *mumble mumble*."

"What's it gonna be, Annie?" I waited.

The woman could do silence better than anyone I'd ever met, even guys in Special Forces. Maybe it was just her silence that rubbed me the wrong way. Most women I'd known only stopped yammering if my cock was in their mouths.

She stood up, pushing her chair back. "I'll take my chances with Evie."

I had to practically chase her back to Dom's. For a slight woman, she had a powerful motor. She didn't even hold the elevator for me, after charming the doorman. My frustration was rising as quickly as I did, all the way up to the penthouse.

When the doors opened, she was standing right there—easy to catch up to. *Easy to catch.* I opened my mouth to ask her why she wasn't going in, until the sound effects echoed down the travertine hallway.

"You want me to lick that sweet pussy, don't you?"

I heard Evie moan in response.

"Beg me, baby. Beg for my cock. If you're a good

girl I'll let you have it—any way you want," my brother promised.

"Jesus, Dom. Have some dignity," I muttered, rubbing the back of my neck. There was pussy-whipped, and then there was pussy-flayed. Thank god I had more self-control than that. Well, mostly.

Annie let out a shaky breath beside me. Her pink lips were parted, her eyes closed. And her warm body was frozen to the spot.

When I inched closer, she didn't move—but she bit her lower lip.

Hmmm.

"You still want to stay here?" I asked in a low voice. Then something shockingly arousing occurred to me. "Are you a voyeur, Annie? Tell me, does it turn you on to listen to them?"

She gasped so quietly I almost didn't hear her. *Almost.*

"Yeah, I think you do. You wish someone's tongue was in your pussy. I bet you're getting wet just thinking about it."

Fuck, I was getting hard thinking about her thinking about it. I moved closer to her side, my chest rubbing up against her shoulder.

Her eyes flew open, but she stared straight ahead. "I-I-uh…"

"If I reached into your pants right now, what would I feel? I'm betting you don't have any panties on."

At the thought, more than just my chest rubbed against her. My cock felt like it was forged from steel. The tiny shake of her head made me grin.

"Bad girl, Annie."

I cupped her breast through her loose cotton top, the

swollen tip of her nipple pressing against my palm. It was a rash, reckless thing to do—but she didn't stop me. It wasn't the first time I'd copped a feel, but this was the first time my hand tingled all the way up my arm.

"Fuck, yes!" Evie cried out.

Apparently Dom's tongue was hard at work. My mouth felt dry, and I swallowed hard.

Annie had leaned closer to me without realizing, turning her body toward me until only a couple of inches separated us. My dick surged in my jeans, instinctively seeking her—her heat, the flat plane of her belly, the warm, damp path down to her entrance. I thumbed her taut nipple, my hand curving around the underside of her tit.

"Jake, I—" she breathed, sucking in a breath when my fingers slid down to the waistband of her borrowed PJs.

I paused, waiting to see what she'd do. What she'd say.

When no reproach was forthcoming, I was emboldened to discover how she'd feel. How she'd taste and smell.

A whimper drifted over her lower lip as I slipped my hand under the hem of her soft shirt and brushed against her even softer skin.

Slowly, my fingertips skated over the quivering purgatory of flesh between her navel and the top of her mound.

The sounds of Dom and Evie making love assaulted our breathy silence. It was as if we mutually understood that speaking would shatter the moment. The heated path on her skin scalded my fingers, until only the dampness of her arousal could bring relief—or so I thought.

"Yes…" she hissed quietly as my index finger parted her lips below a delicate patch of hair. Her head lolled back, her pulse visibly jumping in her long neck. "Jake—"

Was it a warning? A demand to stop? I hesitated, painfully aware of her turgid, slippery clit under my finger.

Oh fuck.

She was throbbing, but our only point of physical connection was my hand in her goddamn pants and our breath on each other's faces.

Until she grabbed my wrist.

My stomach flipped. With a sigh, I began to pull away—but she panted and urged me closer.

"No. *More.*"

Yeah, I did a mental fist pump. What kind of red-blooded man wouldn't?"

"You are *so wet.*" I could smell her desire like a cloud between us as I dipped my finger into her.

In the other room, Evie's guttural cries signaled that she was close to coming. Judging by the curses Dom was snarling, he was trying to get her there before he shot into her.

Annie's head lolled to the side, her slightly almond-shaped eyes dark and wide as she my gaze directly.

My stoicism—hell, my motherfucking patience— was at an end.

ANNIE

$\mathscr{I}$ had never been so turned on in my entire life —and I was wearing pajamas covered in puppies.

"What is it, Annie?" Jake whispered in my ear. "You want more? More fingers? You want me to fuck you with my hand, until even the spaces between my fingers are slippery with your come?"

Yes, please!

As his words grew dirtier, his caresses lightened. His forefinger circled my entrance, nudging just enough for my muscles to spasm in an effort to lure him inside.

"I can't really blame a guy for wanting you," he said. "You're kind of addictive—you know that? You're like... I don't know... eating fresh pineapple."

"Pine-a-apple?" I stuttered.

He hummed. "It's so fresh and juicy and sweet. It's like eating sunshine, and you feel like you just can't get enough—until you eat so much that your mouth burns afterward."

"I-I-" I licked my lips. "I'm burning you?"

"Honey, I'm damn close to going off like a firecrack-er," he admitted.

I shivered as he bent over and ran his tongue from the base of my throat up to my jaw. His finger dragged over my clit at the same time.

My hips jerked and rolled. "Oh god, I'm going to—no, I *can't*!" Sweat broke out at my temples as I struggled against my desires.

"Let it happen, Annie."

I shook my head, frightened by the idea of losing control—even in pleasure. The truth was that I'd already lost that battle; we still stood in the foyer.

Jake's hand moved between my legs, his breath was hot in my ear, and my pants were halfway down my thighs.

His thick wrist flexed as I clutched at him.

"You wanna help?" he asked, his own breath shaky. I looked down at the prominent bulge nudging my hip. My hand brushed against him, and I was shocked by the heat and heft hidden by his clothes.

His groan took me by surprise. Did I think I was the only one affected here, that this was some kind of one-sided seduction?

"I can't take that kind of help." He tilted his hips away from me. "I don't want to embarrass myself."

Of course, it was perfectly fine for me to be embar-rassed. My face felt as hot as the rest of my body. His lips on my cheekbone and the corner of my open mouth didn't cool me down.

"I'm going to make you come so hard," he promised. "You'll feel so damn good. Just stop fighting it."

My gaze shifted to his hand undulating against me,

in me. The fleshy mound below his thumb was shiny with my juices.

His jaw was tight with the strain of holding his own pleasure back, his lips pressed together in concentration, and his gaze penetrated me just as mercilessly as his fingers.

I knew—somehow—that if I told him to stop he would. He'd step back and then… well, that part I didn't know. Lick his fingers, maybe? That realization was enough for me to stop pushing down the intense pleasure trying to travel through my body.

So I stopped fighting my shocking, primal need for him. Hell, I embraced it like it was coming home for the holidays. Sagging against him, I nodded.

"Please, Jake. I-I really want—oh oh *oh!*" I lost my ability to form real words as he drove me over the edge.

He held me together as I shattered, mending my broken pieces with his own harsh exhalation and soft cursing.

Probably, I wasn't the only one with damp pants at that moment. That helped me feel less… exposed and vulnerable—knowing that his self-control had also wavered.

Was I embarrassed? Yes. Yes, I definitely was.

It didn't help that the sound of someone clearing their throat snapped my attention over to Evie and Dominic, now dressed, leaning against the hallway wall.

Watching us.

Evie's eyes shone, but Dom's expression was inscrutable.

Oh my god. I tipped over the edge from embarrassment to utter mortification, faster than I'd climaxed.

Jake chuckled in my ear. "You still want to take your

chances here?" The tip of his tongue touched my earlobe, like he couldn't resist tasting me.

He withdrew his hand and tugged my pants back up. With his hands around my waist, he turned us so that I couldn't see my best friend and her fiancé.

"Looks like you're between a rock and a hard place," he said. "Stay here, or stay with me."

"I could go ho—"

My alternative proposal was shot down by his lips on mine.

Finally.

He kissed me hard—hot and demanding—and it took me a split second to remember that this was the first time.

Our first kiss.

In some ways, it was a step backwards from his... well, his finger fucking me. In other ways it was a mile ahead in terms of intimacy. I was falling and waiting for him to catch me.

Now *this* was the control I feared losing most.

His head lifted slightly. "Here or with me," he repeated. Those were apparently the only options.

Hoo boy. Should I take the rock or the hard place?

~

"The mattress is on the firm side," Jake told me as I sat on the edge of the bed. He shrugged. "It hasn't been used much."

I tilted my head. "You don't have house guests?"

Jake's condo was smaller than his brother's, but I was willing to bet that his en suite bath was still bigger than my whole studio apartment. The minimalist design made it seem even bigger—all straight lines and unforgiving surfaces.

"Not ones that stay in the guest bedroom." His grin showed all his straight, white teeth.

I held up a hand. "Sorry I asked."

I really, *really* was. Jake was a bit of a player—I'd guessed that much. But it was kind of tacky of him to remind me of that after fingering me into a rocketing orgasm. "Your business is your business."

"I mean that Stella has her own room."

"Oh." There was an awkward pause between us. "Can I see it?"

"Her room?"

I nodded. It was stupid of me to ask, but I kind of wanted to see it. How would a single man like Jake—a cocky, wealthy, ex-military man—decorate his toddler daughter's bedroom?

He led me down the hall and opened a door. I looked at his face, wondering if I was being too intrusive, but he didn't seem fazed at all.

I peeked inside. Smiled.

Stella had a princess bed. Not the floofy pink kind but an old-fashioned kind with heavy embroidered curtains around it. It was the kind of bed you saw in old castles, where you'd be surprised at how small it was. It was the perfect size for a three year-old, though. But something was off…

"No little stairs?"

"I don't want her falling in the middle of the night if she gets out," he explained. He rubbed the back of his neck, frowning. "We're working on potty training."

That was definitely a sentence I never expected to hear coming out of Jake Stone's mouth. Judging by the way his ears were turning pink, it was a surprise to him as well.

"That's some pick-up line."

He laughed. "Hey, sometimes dirty talk is literally *dirty talk*."

"Aw, can't wait to be done with the diapers, huh?" I teased.

My gaze swept around the room, taking in a dollhouse, bookshelf, and a neat stack of paper and crayons on a fun-sized table and chair set.

Draped over the back of one of the chairs was a dress. It took me a moment to realize that it was an Elsa costume from the movie *Frozen*.

Everything was too tidy.

"How often is she here?" I asked quietly.

"Not often enough." His voice was tight. He stepped back into the hallway. The tour was over. So was the joking mood.

Damn. As attractive as the intense, provocative Jake was, I liked the devil-may-care part of him more. Right now, he could use more caring than from just the devil. Loneliness shrouded him when he wasn't kidding around.

As we walked to the open-plan kitchen and living room, I poked his arm. "Admit it. You know all the lines in *Frozen*, don't you?"

The tension in his jaw eased up a bit as he grunted, but not enough.

Hmmm. "Who do you think is hotter? Elsa or Anna?"

Silently, he opened the fridge. "Beer or wine?" was all he said.

"Wine, if you have a bottle open."

He nodded. The broad muscles of his back shifted

tantalizingly under his t-shirt as he reached for some glasses. As he was getting them down from the cabinet, his gaze shifted to a framed picture of Stella on the counter by his phone charger.

His shoulders slumped.

This was going to take some industrial-scale making a fool out of myself. I took a deep breath then began to sing—badly.

"The snow glows bright on the mountaintop—"

"Tonight," he interrupted, turning back to me to place the glasses on the island between us.

"What?" *Tonight, what?*

"The snow glows *white* on the mountain *tonight*," he corrected. He looked at Stella's picture again, like a reflex.

Okaaaay. It was worth trying again, just to get a smile on his face again. I took a deep breath.

"Let it go, let it go…" *Shit.* I was flat—in so many ways.

He cocked his head, his lip twitching. "Can't hold it back anymore…"

Fresh arousal snaked up my spine. Somehow he made the Disney musical sound like dark, dirty, sexy rock and roll.

"Let it go, let it go," I warbled as he poured two glasses of white wine. Those were the only words I really knew.

The lines on Jake's face relaxed as stared into my eyes. He paused, searching me for… something, then sang to me in a low, husky voice.

"Don't let them in, don't let them see. Be the good girl you always have to be… Conceal, don't feel; don't let them know. Well now they know…" he trailed off, as though prompting me to repeat the chorus.

I couldn't.

The words he sang stabbed me in the chest right where my heart was supposed to be. They were too true, too close to home.

Struck dumb, I wrapped my fingers around my glass then whirled around to stumble toward the couch. Took a long drink.

Then another.

On the floor by a huge television, I spied the disc case for the movie. Either he had a lazy housekeeper, or he'd been watching it by himself.

Jake Stone was a lot more complicated than I thought he was. And my life was already complicated enough.

My brain knew this.

My body was clueless. It wanted him, more and more every time I saw him.

But my heart was getting stuck between the rock and hard place.

ANNIE

I couldn't move. I fought the rising panic and tried to regulate my breathing, but I still. Could. Not. Move.

"Good, you're awake."

The voice was rough and masculine, but without the ability to even turn my head, I couldn't place it.

Had to breathe. My chest hurt, like something heavy was on it.

When I looked down, I was horrified to see that I was wearing the outfit that had arrived on my doorstep —well, half of it, anyhow. The matching bra and panties didn't quite fit; the cups were too big and the waistband tight.

I lay shivering on the... bed? Couch? *Where the hell was I?*

Frozen. I was frozen. I tried to scream, but couldn't even part my lips.

"I'd offer you a blanket," the voice said, "but I like seeing your nipples stick out like that."

The flush of embarrassment drove away some of my

frigid fear, but not much.

I flinched as, from behind me, he viciously pinched the headlights I still sported. The reactive jerk of my chin and elbows was a relief, though. I was regaining some control over my body!

"But I suppose," he said with regret, "that won't do for the pictures."

In what seemed like a flash, the gown was on me. Long, white satin, it resembled a negligee more than a dress. My shoulders were bare, but the silky material brushed against my ankles.

Then I felt the weight on my chest increase, and my whole body felt like it was caving in on itself. I couldn't stop my eyelids from drooping, and in my mind I was clenching my hands into fists. Then, darkness—like he'd snuffed out a candle inside me.

When I woke again, I was sitting in a big armchair, my hands neatly folded in my lap. They looked strange. *When had I gotten a manicure?*

"You look exquisite." The voice came from behind me. "It turned out perfectly. Don't you think?"

A picture landed on my lap, in a heavy silver frame. My gaze slid up the image from the bottom, as I recognized the gown I was wearing.

But it wasn't me. It was a wedding picture of Evie and Dominic. *What?* I didn't understand.

"Annie!"

At first I felt paralyzed again, then my whole body tensed. My hands flew out to brace me against the bed, as though as I had just fallen backwards.

The bed? Wasn't I in a chair?

I jack-knifed up, nearly head-butting Jake.

"Whoa!"

Looking down, I saw the tank top and underwear I went to sleep in. After the tour. After the impromptu concert. After the wine. After…

Jake gripped my hand where it clawed against the mattress. "Bad dream?"

I looked at him, still trying to focus. Nodded. My ribs ached as though someone had been sitting on them.

"Breathe, honey," he instructed.

Oh. Dreaming. I'd been dreaming that I was Evie? Or was it me? And who was the faceless man, my secret admirer?

"You're cold," Jake said.

I looked down to my nipples poking out through my tank. Broken flashes of the dream skipped through my mind, like a strobe light.

The weight of Jake's thigh, where he sat on the edge of the bed beside me, grounded me. Warmed me.

It wasn't warm enough.

He grunted in surprise as I launched myself at him. He was big, hard, and hot, and swiftly enclosed me in the circle of his arms.

"Hey, hey." One of his hands stroked up and down my spine, the other keeping a similar rhythm on my upper arm. This was the father in him coming out, the protector and soother. *Lucky Stella.* "Must have been some fucking dream," he said.

Presumably that wasn't what he would say to comfort his daughter. I turned my face into his bare chest, my heart racing.

"Shit, even your nose is cold!"

He chuckled and held me tighter. My nose flattened against his pectoral muscle, my short, hot breaths trapped by the curve of my upper lip.

He smelled… warm. Like hot, sugary tea. Despite only wearing some skintight boxer briefs, he radiated heat like a furnace.

Wait, boxer briefs? "I woke you," I realized out loud.

My head joggled along with his shrug. "I wasn't sleeping much anyhow."

"Evie—" I mumbled.

"Yeah, I'd have nightmares after seeing that X-rated scene, too," he joked.

I shook my head slightly, not knowing how to explain. The tip of my nose was warming up, but his back arched a little as my lips brushed against him.

Huh.

Curious, I pursed my lips together again and pressed them to his chest just above his nipple. It stiffened. The muscles of his six-pack flexed as well, as I dragged my hands over his abdomen.

"Annie, what are you doing?" There was a warning in his voice.

I tilted my head back to look at him. "Is it ever hard for you, to see your brother and Evie like that?"

His expression hardened, at least. "Like what?"

"Together." I searched for the right word. "Happy."

"Fucking like bunnies?"

My cheeks heated. "No, more like… they have each other. That kind of intimacy with someone."

Jake disentangled himself and stood up from the edge of the bed. Looked down at me. Any intimacy we'd shared just now was gone, shuttered and put away.

"Annie, I can fuck someone anytime I want."

"That's not what I mean," I said.

I felt the cold return as he moved away. Pushing down the covers, I got on my knees on the bed and crawled closer to him. It was stupid to push him, but when I came to this man I started out a little crazy.

"Don't you ever get lonely?" I wasn't simply curious. I wanted to know if felt like I did.

"Lonely," he echoed.

I couldn't quite see his eyes; he was in silhouette from the light in the hallway outside the bedroom. He folded his arms over his chest, like he was ready for a fight. His chin bobbed up and down as his gaze slid over me.

My tank top and panties were not the kind of armor I was used to doing battle in. I was acutely aware that he was in his underwear, too.

Now that he was standing up and a little above me, the bulge in his briefs was conspicuous. Completely casual about it, he didn't say anything as his cock hardened and grew.

Like a primal, instinctive reaction, my belly squirmed and I felt myself dampen and loosen inside with arousal.

"I'm lonely," I confessed.

It was hard to say that, but it was so goddamn true. Saying it out loud made me feel lonelier, if that was possible.

I sighed, dropping back down to sit on my heels, my hands on my thighs. Nothing had changed by admitting it, other than feeling worse and making a fool out of myself—again. In my attempt to push him into revealing more of himself, I'd fallen flat on my face.

Then Jake dropped his arms, his hands curling into fists at his side. His head lolled back and he sighed heavily. "Fuck, Annie."

Yeah, fuck Annie.

"You're killing me, here." He stepped toward the bed. "You know it's not a good idea."

"Why not?" I shriveled inside with a humiliating, depressing thought. "Is it because of Evie?"

"What about Evie?"

"Are you still in love with her?"

His mouth opened, then closed. "What the fuck are you talking about? I was never in love with her."

Well, that didn't make me feel any better.

His frown deepened. "Not that it's any of your business, but it was a… thing. We needed and wanted each other at that time." He passed his hand over his face so I couldn't see his eyes as he continued. "That brief, fucking time. It was a little crazy and maybe—probably —a bad idea, now that I think about it. But Annie, we were—*are*—adults."

"So am I. An adult, I mean. Unless you're not attracted to me…" I only felt comfortable saying that, because I knew it wasn't true.

Even if it weren't for the giant erection bobbing in front of my face, Jake was still a *man*. As a general rule, men didn't usually turn down women falling at their feet.

Then again, Jake was exceptional.

Silently, he met my gaze as he rubbed his hands over the short hair on his head. There was empathy in his eyes. Accusation. Arousal. What did he see in me?

"I'm trying to be a gentleman," he finally said, "and you're making it really hard."

I crawled over to him, my gaze fixed on his erection. My heart raced. "What if I don't want you to be a gentleman?"

It startled me when he cupped my chin. "Annie, I'm not a relationship kind of guy."

I recoiled. "Did I ask for a ring? It could just be... I don't know, a pity fuck."

Sayonara, self-esteem. It was nice knowing you.

I couldn't believe that I was trying to convince him. I had a stalker, for God's sakes! I wasn't unappealing, or desperate. I was just very, very turned on.

Jake put his knee on the bed and dropped down over me. I reared back, falling on my ass and bracing myself on my elbows underneath him.

"You are *not* a pity fuck." His eyes—his whole body—blazed, but he didn't touch me. "You deserve to be worshipped. You should have every inch of your body sucked on like a candy cane. But I'm not the guy to do it."

I spread my legs to cradle him as he hovered over me then craned my neck up to kiss the bristle of beard under his jaw. The insides of my knees touched his lean hips.

"Annie..." His muscles tensed under my mouth as our bodies made contact.

"I think." I tasted my way down his neck. "You are." Nipped at his throbbing carotid artery. "The perfect person to do it."

His plank position sagged, until his hard, hot cock pressed against the damp crotch of my panties.

We both groaned.

"Jesus," he breathed, dropping his face into the curve between my neck and shoulder. "I was wrong. You *are* a ninja."

"Show me," I whispered into his ear. "Show me how

I should be fucked, because your fingers weren't enough. I need you to fill me, Jake."

Until there was no room in my head for fear or anxiety or self-doubt. Until I felt truly safe.

There was something irresistible about knowing I could give up control with him. I wouldn't have to be strong all the time; he could hold me up and take care of me. I'd never had that, and the thought was intoxicating.

His lips found my earlobe, sending ticklish sparks down my neck. Slowly he began rocking against me, every nudge making me wetter with wanting him.

"I am *not* in love with Evie," he said firmly.

I nodded. "I believe you." *Now.*

"I don't fall in love."

Something squeezed inside me. "I-I believe you. Neither do I."

Never had, never would. I just wanted… comfort, connection, and to come with another person—for once. It was harder for two people to be lonely together, right?

Tingling sensations spread over my skin with every brush of his chest against mine. I tucked my feet around him, luxuriating in the crispness of the hair on his legs against my inner thighs. Under the soles of my feet.

He rose up, his heavy-lidded gaze searching mine. "This would just be us fucking, not falling in love."

"Fine."

"I won't be gentle." When I stilled, he clarified, "I won't treat you like glass. You're the one who attacked me in the dark, remember? You can take it."

"Got it." I nodded solemnly. "Must fuck back." I

could do that. I wriggled against him, trying to get him to rub *right there*.

Jake's grin transformed his face. "Okay, then, Annie."

I barely had time to inhale before he captured my mouth in a ravenous kiss. He took my breath, and in return gave me the strength to beg for more.

"Soon," he promised when I whimpered.

After another sweep of his lips against mine, he rose up on his knees and shoved down the waistband of his briefs. He curled his fingers in the damp crotch of my panties, pulling them to the side.

Was he going to enter me… right now?

"Foreplay?" I panted.

"What the hell do you think we've been doing?" he asked me, dipping his first two fingers into my core.

"Ungh!" I arched my back. "I said your fingers weren't enough!"

"Oh, we're just getting started." With a smirk, he twisted his hands on either side of the seam of my underwear and ripped.

My mouth fell open. "I could have just taken them off, you know."

"Waste of time." He scooted back a few inches and dropped his chest to the bed between my legs.

I liked those panties. *Damn*. "Maybe those had senti-mental value." I pouted.

"Seriously?" He snorted. "Those are disposable."

"My *underwear*?" Where the hell did he think I shopped?

"Sentimental values. Besides, I think that turned you on," he guessed, his eyebrow lifting.

It sure did. The sight of his head between my legs made me breathless.

I moaned when he slid his thumb into me. I writhed when he tried to see how many fingers he could fit in me at once. His left hand splayed over my belly, while his right hand spread me open to expose my clit. When he finally took me in his mouth, I almost began to sob.

"Oh fuck! Jake!"

His tongue slid over me, lapping and curling and tracing at the tip. He may not have treated me like glass, but he fulfilled his promise to suck me like a piece of candy.

"When was the last time someone ate you out, Annie?"

I tossed my head from side to side on the bed, not knowing. Not caring.

"Answer me," he demanded, lashing at a particularly sensitive spot.

Looking down at him, I decided to be honest. I owed him no less. "Never? Definitely not like this."

He was making me forget my own name, much less any past, polite, pathetic encounters.

"Damn straight," he muttered. "You taste so fucking good. Like butterscotch." He grinned up at me, his mouth and chin shiny.

His palm left my stomach. Before I could react, he wedged his hands under the curve of my butt cheeks and hauled me to his mouth. He drank from me greedily —his lips, tongue, teeth and nose pressing into places that had never been treated with so much… avarice.

I felt like a cartoon character being electrocuted—all my bones stiff and disjointed, and an indefinable halo around my body. The shadow of his beard rasped over my raw nerve endings, followed by the liquid fire of his tongue.

A ball of lightning rolled up in my belly, sending an expectant ache through my center.

"Oh! Jake, I'm—"

"I know. It's okay. *Let it go.*"

I barked out a laugh. *At least he didn't sing it.*

Lightheaded from anticipation, I floated up to the sky to find my climax. I felt like I was drifting away— away from my feelings, away from fear.

Oh yes… Almost there…

As though he couldn't bear to lose his tether on me, Jake clutched me in his hands, spreading me wider. His tongue dove into my still quivering pussy, his teeth fastened lightly on my clit, and his thumbs pressed together to gently nudge at my sensitive rear entrance. The combined sensations brought me back to earth.

No longer the reluctant, guilty predator, he gleefully possessed me and made sure that I knew I was at his mercy. He gave and took in equal measure. He didn't treat me like glass, but I sang and cracked like crystal nonetheless.

I screamed. My ascent was subverted, like he'd tugged on the string of my balloon and brought me back down to the rough and raw reality of our fucking. I wasn't allowed to drift far away. He worked me over as I came—hard.

And then the balloon popped, and he caught me.

JAKE

I'd had a lot of new experiences in my life.

As an orphan and foster kid.

As an adopted brother to "Richie Rich."

As a military man.

As a father.

But I'd never had a woman sleep in my bed.

Wait. Technically, since this was my guest bedroom, I still hadn't. *Yes!* My streak held!

I'd never been a good sleeper. A fractured childhood, nightmares, a lonely mansion and competitive adolescence, basic training, learning how to run a business—they all contributed to restless nights.

It wasn't until I woke up beside Annie that I realized I'd actually *slept* with her. Unconsciously. Subconsciously.

Basically, we'd fucked ourselves into exhaustion. There was no clock in this bedroom, but the thin halo of light around the blinds probably meant it was early morning. So, I'd slept maybe three or four hours, which was usually enough for me.

I could go work out. I could fuck around on my phone. I could do lots of things, but instead I stared at Annie.

She was just so damn… interesting. Sure, she was beautiful, in an exotic, pocket-sized way. Cute, even. A human Tamagotchi pet.

Shit, that was a bad example.

But it wasn't just her looks that captured my attention. Even the way she came fascinated me. It was like she needed my permission, even my command, to let the feelings take over. Then I became a selfish, jealous motherfucker and wanted to be part of every single second of her pleasure. After all, it was because of me, right?

When she begged for my cock, it was a no-brainer. She'd needed me earlier, and I was only too happy to help her out with that. It took a lot for her to tell me that she was lonely; I knew just how that felt.

Now I felt more confused than before.

Sex was usually the *end* of my brief relationships—if you could even call them that—with women. The longest I'd spent with one woman was with Stella's mom.

On darker days I wondered where I'd be if I'd gotten out earlier. There wouldn't be a bed down the hall that looked like it was stolen from a midget Medieval Times, at least. There were moments when I fantasized about that, then felt guilty as fuck for even imagining life without my little star.

Becoming a father, even part-time, made me realize just how fucked up the world was. Yeah, foster care and the service didn't do that. Not even knowing Dom and his Grandad prepared me for the surreal experience of parenting.

Three years in, I was finally getting a grip on things —and Annie had gone and pried all my goddamn fingers apart.

The woman dead to the world in front of me was a bundle of contradictions, like a ball of tangled rubber bands. I was pretty confident that she'd bounce if I dropped her, but fuck if I knew which way she'd go.

I'd never before met a woman who made me want to ask so many questions.

Usually the questions I asked hot women were precursors to getting them into bed. Where did you go to school, what's your dream job, did you have a pet growing up—panty-dropping bullshit like that. Shallow, fake conversations to provide a thin veneer of social interaction before pulling out a strip of rubbers.

Shit. Shit shit fuck.

I'd forgotten a condom with Annie.

My eyes narrowed at her, like it was her fault that I'd been irresponsible. I was the idiot, though. It wasn't fair of me to blame her for my mistake, when she was completely dickmatized herself. She'd still been coming, her tight walls still rippling from her orgasm, when I rose up and slammed into her.

She'd cried out, making me pause and second-guess myself, before digging her heels into my ass and pulling me deeper into her. "Oh god, I'm so *full!*"

I hadn't wanted to hurt her with my generous cock but, well… I was a generous kind of guy. "Am I hurting you, honey? You're so fucking tight."

My whole soul felt like it was in a vise.

"No, no. It's fine," she panted, her forehead furrowing as I slowly moved back and forth.

My aching dick wanted to take her at her word. I'd

managed to hang on while I was kissing her, eating her out. At one point I realized this was what middle-aged men on Viagra felt. I'd been fighting with my erection all fucking day—or at least it seemed that way.

Now I was balls-deep in her heat, and I didn't want to leave. "Annie, I want to fuck you so badly." My hips jerked, making her moan.

"Jacob Stone," she said sternly, "if you fuck me *badly*, I will never forgive you."

I chuckled then groaned when I felt her giggles on the inside. "Jesus, Annie. How many mind-blowing orgasms does one woman need?"

"Is that a rhetorical question?"

"Is that a challenge?" When she bit her lip, I thrust a little deeper. *Oh yeah*. "Mission accepted."

And then I proceeded to fuck her brains out.

It didn't take long before I was yelling and arching my back as I shot into her.

I waited for her to come first, of course. And second.

But then I couldn't wait any longer, and the coil of tension within me sprang open.

I fell on my back beside her, breathless. Damn, she was still too far away. She was staring at the ceiling as I pulled her into my side.

"Mind blown?" I asked like an arrogant moth-erfucker.

Her mouth opened and closed like a goldfish. It would have been really funny if my brain didn't go to other, dirtier places as she pursed her lips.

Even now, fast asleep, her lips parted a little when she breathed. I wanted to lean over and test if the tip of my tongue would fit in that space, wanted to put my ear to her mouth to see if she was very, very quietly snoring.

She sighed in her sleep, startling me. How long had I been staring at her? My phone buzzed, drawing my attention away from the woman in my bed—my *guest* bed.

After a few words on the phone with the security desk downstairs, I exhaled heavily and slid out of bed. All I could find on the floor to put on were my discarded briefs, so I hurried to my bedroom.

The rapping at the door nearly caused a tragic accident as I zipped up a pair of jeans. Jesus, I was jumpy.

"Okay, okay," I grumbled.

Another series of knocks rattled my nerves. I stalked through the living room and yanked open the door.

"You know I'm here. Why do you keep knocking?"

My ex lifted a penciled-in eyebrow. "I thought maybe you'd gone back to sleep."

"Oh, for fu—" I remembered the toddler nudging Sheila's knee. "*Fun*'s sake. When I'm up, I'm up."

"I remember," she said as Stella migrated from her mother's leg to mine. Sheila's gaze slid over my body, and I regretted not grabbing a shirt.

"Daddy!"

When I looked down at my daughter, the irritation rippling in my chest flattened out, like the sea after a storm. All that was left was bubbles from the violent waves and a vague sense of nausea. Even that dissipated when she smiled at me.

"Hi, baby." Automatically, I hauled her up on my hip. I knew she hated it when everyone spoke above her head. My little girl didn't like being towered over.

"You gotta stop picking her up all the time," Sheila rebuked.

I shrugged. It wasn't the first time we'd had this

exchange, and I couldn't care less. I'd take my daughter in my arms whenever the fuck I wanted to.

"What's the deal?" I asked.

"I had a job interview a few days ago, and they asked me to come in for the morning shift to shadow somebody."

"At dark o'clock?" Reflexively I turned my gaze to the hallway, wondering if we'd woken up Annie. I didn't hear anything. *Good.*

"It's with emergency dispatch. Nine-one-one."

I frowned. "Can you take that kind of job, with her?" I jerked my chin toward Stella. Her blonde curls tickled my jaw, smelling a little like honey. "That can be pretty shit—" Sheila glared. *Right, the fucking swear jar.* "Shifty hours. Shift work."

"I'll figure it out. It's a great opportunity."

Saying nothing, I reveled in the smell of my baby's hair. "How long?"

She shook her head as she dug into her giant tote bag. "Few hours, maybe? I'll text you."

There was nothing else to say. Sheila never asked; she just assumed I'd be there. Mostly, I was. There were times when it rankled that not only did she take it for granted that I'd come to the rescue, but that I always proved her right.

We both knew that I'd never let Stella down, and Sheila used it to her advantage.

I glared at her, but her attention was focused on her phone. "You could have called first."

"They *just* called me. I didn't want to blow them off," she explained—like it was no big deal to get a toddler up before the sun and drag her out. Had she given her breakfast, even?

I looked down at Stella, unable to carbon date the dried chocolate milk mustache around her mouth.

Sheila wasn't a bad mother, not at all.

When she first told me she was pregnant, my first thought was "gold-digger." Actually, my knee-jerk response was "Are you sure it's mine?" but if I hadn't stopped the words from coming out of my mouth, I might not have been able to father future children.

But when we'd gone our separate ways, she'd surprised me by telling me that she didn't want money. Yeah, I made sure they didn't need anything, but Sheila *liked* working. She put most of the child support I gave her in a bank account for Stella.

Even when she lived with me, when we tried to make it work, she didn't want handouts.

I couldn't really complain about that.

I'd done most of my complaining about the dude she fucked in the apartment when Stella was only about six months old.

All moms need a break, sure. But I thought she'd go for brunch or go shopping or something—not go down on a stranger on my bed.

At that point, it had already been a long six months since Stella was born. If I'd thought living with a woman took some getting used to, it was nothing to living with a baby.

Strangely, though, it took me a long time to get used to the quiet again, after I got them a new apartment. Also the new mattress, since I sent my contaminated bed with her.

"You need anything?" she asked, holding up a couple of pull-up diapers.

"I'm good." I had everything that my daughter needed. All the time. Always.

Hugs and kisses later—between her and Stella, not me—she left and I carried my shooting star into the kitchen.

"Real, Daddy?"

Cereal. "Sure, baby. Want the noisy kind?"

She bounced in my arms. Her giggles at the snap, crackle and pop always made me smile.

I found the box of Rice Krispies and a plastic bowl for her, then set her down on a booster seat and snapped the belt shut around her waist so she didn't topple over.

Should I make breakfast for Annie? How long was she going to sleep? I washed Stella's face, rinsed her cereal bowl and threw it in the sink, then got some eggs and a frying pan out.

"Elsa!" Stella squatted by the TV, a DVD case in her hands.

"Not right now." I took the case from her ridiculously strong grip.

"I want Elsa and Anna!"

"Jesus, kid. Let it go," I muttered. "I said, 'not now.'" I put the television on for her, and went back to the kitchen to consider the eggs. Scrambled? Poached?

Who was I kidding? Any attempt I made at something else ended up in scrambled, anyhow.

I was whisking the eggs with a fork when I heard a scream.

ANNIE

*O*f all the ways a person can be woken up, a toddler two inches away from your face is not the most peaceful. My reflexive screech scared the shit out of both of us. Wide-eyed, the two-foot terror tumbled back onto the floor beside the bed.

Jake burst through the doorway, his expression ferocious. He halted, sagging when he saw me. His gaze immediately softened when it moved to Stella.

"You okay?"

Was he addressing me, or his daughter? She was on the floor, but looked no worse for it. Besides, at her age she was already a lot closer to the floor. I, on the other hand, had just about suffered a heart attack.

"Who dat?"

"Annie," Jake said.

She popped up and beamed at me. "On a delsa?"

I turned to Jake, not fluent in Toddler.

He grinned at me. At least, in the direction of my bare neck, shoulders, and upper chest. His x-ray vision already knew what my breasts looked like under the quilt I clutched to me.

"Not like Anna and Elsa, starlight," he explained. "Her name's Annie. And right now we should give her some privacy." He reached for Stella's hand and tugged her to the door. "Why don't you help me crack some more eggs?" He rolled his eyes at me. "After I clean up the ones on the floor."

"Where her jammies?" Stella demanded.

I pulled the blanket over my mouth, trying not to laugh. Jake searched me for an answer. I blinked in response. Like I knew? I went to bed with a tank top on, but had no idea where it'd ended up. My torn panties were on the floor somewhere—at least Stella hadn't discovered those.

With his hand on Stella's golden head and his smirk pointed at me, he prodded her out of sight. "Uh, she lost them."

"Is she cold?"

As they disappeared down the hall, I heard Jake reply, "No, I don't think she's cold at all."

Alone once more, I drew my knees up and rested my chin on them. No, I hadn't been cold last night in Jake's arms.

Part of me was still embarrassed by the loneliness I'd shared with him. Another part of me was still sore from the remedy.

As predicted, my panties were a lost cause. I found my tank and the skinny jeans I was wearing yesterday, at least. Going commando might be okay for guys, but it made me wince in discomfort. *Ugh.*

When I walked out to the kitchen, the sight of Jake bent over Stella while she focused on the eggs made me smile. He didn't seem to care that her preferred technique was smashing it on the side of the bowl and letting it drip through her little fingers, shell and all.

When his gaze lifted to me and he grinned, it was like he'd punched me in the chest. "I hope you like your eggs crunchy."

"I… uh…"

Damn. Suddenly my life felt kind of crunchy. What the hell was I doing here?

Six months ago, I was sharing a bottle of wine with Evie and encouraging her to do wild, daring things. I'd sacrificed one of my favorite lingerie sets to the cause, even. But I was, at heart, not that wild or daring. I worked. I kept to myself, mostly. I worked. Sometimes I dated, but after the itch was scratched, I didn't feel the urge to continue.

Now I had a secret admirer, a not-so secret admirer, and a little girl staring at me like she'd never seen a woman in her daddy's kitchen before.

Maybe she hadn't.

"D'you like bacon?" Stella asked.

I blinked at her. "Bacon?"

"Bacon is the bestest. But Daddy burns it." Her little face screwed up in distaste.

Jake shrugged. "It's true. I'm more of a sausage kind of guy."

Oh yeah, was he ever.

"I want bacon!" Stella stomped her foot on the chair she was standing on at the kitchen island then wobbled as she nearly fell. Jake's arms were around her in a flash, righting her.

Holding her.

Securing her.

The memory of those same, strong arms around me made something quiver deep inside. It was a sudden flash of feeling that was more than sexual, more than physical attraction. My gaze traced his embrace, his hands reaching past his daughter to pinch broken pieces of eggshell in the bowl before them.

Jake had a lot going for him—about nine inches, at the very least.

He was hot but he was also warm-hearted, intense but playful, and he wore his heart on his sleeve. Literally, he had a jagged-looking heart tattooed on his left arm. It almost looked like a superhero symbol with a shaky "S" in the middle.

How had I not noticed that before? Probably because I hadn't been looking for a hero. I'd always made a point of rescuing myself.

"I can cook bacon," I announced.

Stella craned her head to beam at her dad. "Daddy! She can do it!"

"I heard, starlight."

Within five minutes, I found myself slicing open a pack of bacon with a pair of kitchen shears. Stella's attention bounced between my actions and the TV, as though she weren't sure which was more critical to keep her eye on.

Jake knelt beside me, retrieving a frying pan from a lower cupboard.

I shook my head. "I need a cookie sheet."

He shoved the pan back in the cupboard, muttering to himself, "Do I have one of those?"

"You've never made cookies with her?"

His broad, bare shoulders shrugged, glancing against my thigh. His head bobbed as he looked in the cupboard. My fingers slid over the greasy strips of bacon, pulling them out and separating them.

"Do you have parchment paper?"

"Honey, I am a single man. You're fucking lucky I have *this*." He slapped a rectangular metal pan on the counter. It looked like a casserole pan of some kind, but it would do. Stella hadn't heard—or hadn't registered—his adult language, having traded the cooking class for TV.

Jake did have tin foil. While I lined the pan with it, I instructed him to turn on the oven.

"I like it when you're bossy," he said.

My hand trembled as I lay out the strips. "Most men don't."

"I'm not most men." His arms circled around me to pin me against the counter.

Heat bloomed over my chest with the sensation of his breath on my bare shoulders, but my nipples hardened as though an ice cube had been touched to them. He stood so close behind me that I felt his erection press into my lower back.

It was hard not to stutter when I said, "Um, sugar?"

I shuddered as he swept my hair over my shoulder so he could nibble on my neck. Oh god, he knew exactly where to touch me, where to taste me.

"Honey?" His tongue dragged over the pulse in my neck. *Could he feel it throbbing?*

"N-no, I need sugar. Brown sugar, if you have it. And chili powder."

"Sweet and spicy. I like it." He hummed his approval, his teeth clamping down gently like a vampire's bite.

Oh god. This was why women shouldn't go without

underwear. The arousal flaring through me threatened to soak through my jeans. His large, hot body trapped me, his hips rocking against me with prurient promise.

Brown sugar and chili powder were too much to ask of a bachelor's pantry, apparently. Jake gave me just enough space to work, while making it almost impossible for me to do it efficiently. My focus atrophied as I improvised with maple syrup and a bit of black pepper.

"You know what's so great about bacon?" he whispered in my ear as I covered it with another sheet of foil. I didn't want the fat spattering in the oven and setting off the smoke alarm.

"What?"

"The way it melts on your tongue. Salty. It can be crispy or chewy, but you can still taste it on your lips for a long time after." He licked my neck. *Oh my...*

It was a surprise that I hadn't gone up in flames yet, with the way that Jake's hands splayed over my hips. His fingers slid into the pockets of my tight jeans, and his thumbs dipped under the waistband. I felt like a human thumbprint cookie, like his touch would leave a mark. Somehow I slid the bacon into the oven without burning myself. It helped that Jake stepped back to let me open and close the door.

Briefly.

"How long?" he asked, spinning me around until we were facing each other.

"Um, we should keep an eye on it." The edge of the counter dug into my back. He was so. Damn. Close. And I *loved* it. "Maybe fifteen, twenty minutes? It depends."

"On what?"

"On how you like it," I said faintly. I tilted my head back to see him lick his lips. His eyes were dark.

He looked hungry—and not for the bacon popping and crackling in the oven behind me. "Bacon is bacon. It's always good."

"Unless you burn it," I pointed out, glancing over at Stella in the living room. She was engrossed in some cartoon.

"I might not be a great cook, Annie, but I'm great in the kitchen."

I hissed as his knuckles brushed against the ticklish skin of my belly. Gasped as he popped open the top button of my jeans. Moaned as his hand dove inside to drag through my damp cleft. Maybe there were some advantages to going commando.

"Holy fuck." My eyes closed as he twisted his hand, plunging two thick fingers into me.

"God, I *wish*. I want you, Annie." His breath was hot against my mouth as he bent over me. "I want to peel these goddamn jeans off you and lift you up on this counter."

I wouldn't mind that. "What else would you do to me?"

"What wouldn't I do?" His chuckle rubbed against all my nerve endings as his fingers curled inside me. "I'd line myself up with your tight pussy and push inside, very, very slowly. Give you time to adjust." He added another finger.

"Considerate of you." I bit my lip.

"I'm that kind of guy."

I frowned. "What if we don't line up this way? What if we didn't, uh, fit?"

I was on sensory overload, close to shorting out like a blown fuse. The scent of the cooking bacon curled around us, the unmistakable sweet, salty, spicy scent penetrating my senses.

"Hmmm." He considered it. "Then I guess I'd just have to spread you open and use my tongue."

Oh god. I could imagine that. I could almost feel it. Warmth suffused me. "That doesn't sound... uh... hygienic."

He sighed. "You're right. I'm dirty."

The curve of his lips told me that he offered no apologies for it. Honestly, I didn't expect any, nor did I really want them.

"I think I like you that way," I confessed.

I only saw a flash of his grin before he captured my mouth, his tongue sweeping inside me as mercilessly as his fingers.

Up and down. Back and forth. He teased me and tortured me, taking me swiftly to the edge of climax.

He raised his head to examine me as I panted. "You gonna come for me, Annie?"

Did I have a choice? I shuddered, my body responding uncontrollably.

"Oh yeah," he growled. "I want to feel that slippery cunt of yours tightening. I fucking *crave* that right now. The bacon has nothing on the scent of your sweet pussy. That's what's making my mouth water."

"I'm better than bacon?" My eyes rolled back— partly in disbelief, but mostly because I was falling apart.

"Honey, I'm pretty confident that I can cook you. Right. *Now*." He rubbed his thumb over my clit while twisting his fingers inside me, and I was done before the bacon.

It wasn't an earth-shaking orgasm. It was a storm surge flooding my senses, filling my body with pleasure.

If his hands weren't holding me steady, I might have slipped off the counter, rolling with the tide.

"That's it. Oh yeah, Annie. You're so gorgeous when you come."

He made me *feel* gorgeous, especially when he kissed me with such tenderness and sweetness. Jake had me all mixed up—beaming with pride, but blushing like a virgin bride on her wedding night.

The heat in my face turned nuclear when I heard Stella begin to sing in the next room.

Oh my god. Had I just let Jake—? While his daughter was twenty feet away?

My hands on his chest, I pushed him backward until his ass bounced off the edge of the island.

He frowned. "What?"

"Stella!" I hissed as I slithered down. My knees wobbled and my fingers fumbled at my jeans as I tried to make myself presentable again. "Seriously? She's right *there*. That was so dumb. So reckless. So—"

"Hot."

My lips parted. "You have no shame, do you?"

"Nope." He snaked his arm around my waist and pulled me to him. His other hand went to my chin to tilt my face up. "Don't get me wrong, Annie. I would never —*never*—do something that would hurt my daughter. Fuck, I don't even date seriously."

My stomach lurched at the reminder. What did that make me? A fling? A fuck buddy? A cock tease?

The substantial bulge pressing against my stomach reminded me that only one of us had been satisfied.

His fingers tightened, his thumb rubbing my bottom lip. "Annie, there is a time and a place for everything." He jerked his head toward the living room. "She's fine.

That's her time and her place—for now. This is ours. If I thought she was even remotely interested in what we—"

"*Daddy!*"

Stella stood beside us, pointing at the smoking oven.

ANNIE

"So are you all moved in?" Evie sat forward, her wine nearly spilling with the sudden movement.

She didn't even flinch when I narrowed my eyes at her.

"It's temporary," I reminded her. "And not exactly my choice."

When she'd arrived at the restaurant to pick me up after work, I was happy to see her—until she announced that she was assigned "security detail." Jake really didn't think I could take care of myself, even enough to get to his place after my shift? Then again, maybe he suspected that I would have just gone back to my apartment.

He would have been right.

Evie's curvy body and bouncy blonde hair was not unwelcome at the restaurant. Darren, the bus boy slash dishwasher, kept sneaking peeks at her before averting his eyes like she was an eclipse. Even John, our uptight manager, softened as Evie's smile contaminated his front of house.

It had been less than a week, but I was getting sick of my own, personal Secret Service. A few days earlier, Jake and his daughter had accompanied me to my apartment so I pick up some personal items.

Stella helped "fold" my clothes as we filled a suitcase. "Now you have jammies!" she reassured me as she packed my only set.

"Don't let her pack your underwear," Jake whispered in my ear.

I raised an eyebrow. "I can't *not* bring underwear." For one thing, it was impractical. For another thing, it was a little, er, messy—especially around him.

He had a dampening effect on my lady bits.

When I said as much to him, he seemed unconvinced that I was a lady. His chuckle sent a little ripple of excitement through me. "I'll be in charge of packing your panties," he said.

"Perv." But I smiled, pointing to the top drawer of a dresser I salvaged and repainted. "Help yourself." He still owed me for the pair he ripped off me.

"What next?" Stella asked.

She was so damn sweet, it made my teeth hurt. I sent her into the bathroom to get my toothbrush.

"And why don't you see what else you think I might need?" I suggested, a little curious about what a three year-old would come up with as essential items.

Beaming at being assigned such an important task, she disappeared into the closet-sized bathroom.

Jake examined my bras—thankfully in the drawer, not the one on my body at that moment. Yep, damp panties. Blushing despite myself, I went in the other room to pack my laptop bag.

When I returned, Stella was still on her toiletry treasure hunt, and her father's eyes had darkened into pools of lust. What exactly was in my top drawer, again?

Silently, he dangled a lace thong from his fingers.

"Definitely pack that," I told him. "In fact, pack *all* of them." I had the feeling I would need extra—not that I even knew how long I'd be held hostage at his place.

He tossed a handful over to the bag on the bed. Looked back and hummed.

"These are sexy." Jake held up my oldest pair of granny panties for when Aunt Flo came to town.

I couldn't tell if he was kidding or serious. "Sentimental value," I said.

Holding my gaze, he twisted his fingers around the worn cotton, and tore a giant hole in the ass with his thumb.

"Oops," he drawled.

My mouth fell open. *Seriously?* "You need to take me shopping," I demanded, crossing my arms over my chest.

"Done!" Stella traipsed back into the room, dumping an armful of stuff on the bed. We all sat down to examine her loot like it was a bag of Halloween candy.

Toothbrush, check. Toothpaste, check. Shampoo and conditioner, check and check. I smiled at Stella. "Good job."

I frowned when I saw my razor. *Shit, she shouldn't have touched that.* Quickly, I snatched it up and moved it out of her reach.

"Daddy uses those on his face. Do you?"

Jake snickered.

"No, sweetie. I use them on my legs, mostly."

"And a few other places," Jake said under his breath, before holding up a maxi pad in bemusement.

"You need diapers?" Stella asked, then confided, "I still pee my pants sometimes, too." Her disappointment in herself was obvious.

Her father's chuckles turned into a laugh, while I just turned bright pink. "It's okay," I said lamely. "Thanks."

If I thought that would be the most embarrassing part of my day, I was sorely mistaken. Jake somehow managed to interrogate every man of my acquaintance that we came in contact with—from the gruff building superintendent to the staff at the restaurant when he dropped me off at work. And he refused to lay off when I asked him to.

"Jake, don't you think that I'd know if this…" 'Secret admirer' sounded too trite, and 'stalker' too scary. "This guy is someone I already know?"

"Why would you rule it out? He probably is. You're pretty irresistible for a short chick with zero martial arts skills."

"You're such a charmer. No wonder Evie likes you," I said, a lump rising in my throat at the reminder of his past with Evie.

I wanted to bring it up with her, so badly. I wanted to ask her what he was like, when she was *with* him.

Jake had told me it was a casual thing, and to drop the subject, but… now, on Evie and Dom's penthouse couch, the thought lay between us like the bottle of cabernet we'd almost finished.

"Jake's such a bachelor," Evie mused. "How's he adjusting?"

"Fine." I wanted to lay claim to him somehow, wanted her to know that I meant more to him than she did—even if I wasn't sure whether it was true, or even if I wanted it to be so. "He said I could redo the bedroom in French Country," I joked.

"So you *are* sleeping with him."

Shit. Well, it wasn't exactly a secret. My friend stared off into the distance while she sipped her wine. A mysterious smile transformed her mouth, like she was the Mona Lisa of ménage.

Yeah, I knew she'd been with Jake and Dom, separately and together. In fact, I'd pushed her to try it, to experiment, to take a chance. Now I wondered if I'd pushed her too far.

"Did he—" I broke off, not sure I wanted to know.

"Did he what?"

"Nothing." I pulled out the collar of my cream button-up shirt, fanning myself against a sudden flash of heat.

"Bullshit. Did he *what*?" Evie had gained a lot of confidence since meeting the Stone brothers. I wished I felt that kind of assurance.

"Did he kiss you a lot?" I asked her quietly, staring at the dregs of wine in my oversized glass.

Jake kissed me more than I… what? Thought he would? Thought he should? Maybe I needed practice. The memory of his taste and his tongue in my mouth made me reach to empty the bottle.

"Annie, are you asking me to kiss and tell?" Evie giggled, her fair skin flushed from the wine. "He's a good kisser, but Dom's better."

Big sip. Bigger eye roll. "I'll take your word for it."

"Dom does this thing at the top of my upper lip—I can't describe it. He kind of does the same thing when he's going down on me, and it just blows my mind." She expanded her fist out, stretching her fingers out in the air.

I sighed.

Silently, Evie put her wine glass down on the coffee table. Then she reached over and stroked my cheek. "I've never seen you blush so much!" she said.

"It's the wine."

"No, it's not. Are you *shy*? Annie, what happened to the woman who chanted 'do it, do it, do it' over the phone when I was thinking about a threesome?"

"I was—oh, I don't know. It doesn't matter. Everyone loves Evie; I get it."

Suddenly it was so clear. I was jealous.

Of course, it had occurred to me before, but I was *really* jealous. And insecure. Evie was all blonde and bust and bubbles, and Jake had clearly been attracted to her at one time. I was so different from her—why would he like me?

"Seriously, Annie? What a dumb thing to say." Evie scooted closer on the couch, until our thighs were touching. "You're gorgeous."

"I'm 'exotic.'" I made air quotes and rolled my eyes.

"You're smart."

"Not as smart as you."

"You've got street smarts, which counts for more in my book."

Clearly nobody had told her about my short-lived career as a ninja.

"But, Evie, you have boobs." I jerked my chin down. "These are barely more than freaking mosquito bites."

Her laugh was so sharp and sudden that she snorted. "See. You're also funny."

Okay, I would concede that.

"Annie, you're sexy. You have to know that."

"Sexy?"

Sure, I felt sexy with Jake. It was hard *not* to feel sexy when you were sucking a beautiful man's brain out through his cock. But the way Evie was staring at me, with clear admiration, made me really think it was true. It was funny how sometimes another woman's opinion meant more.

"You know what I think?" she whispered. I cocked my head. Drank the last sip of wine. "I think that this secret admirer of yours has fucked up your self-esteem."

I choked a little. *Wine was not supposed to go down that way.* I looked down at the red wine I'd just spluttered on my shirt. "Evie, just because I have a stalker doesn't make me worth the stalking."

"You're trying to convince me that you're not sexy because you think it will make this whole situation go away, somehow. But it won't, and you are."

Was she right?

"You just need to believe it, Annie. You think I discovered some great secret of sexual confidence? I didn't. I just started trusting in myself. Experimenting more. And not giving a fuck what anyone else thinks."

Well, I definitely had the last part of that down.

Evie's eyes dropped to my shirt. "Come on, let's get that cleaned up before it stains."

We went to the kitchen, where she grabbed the dish soap and a sponge. "Come on, take it off."

My fingers went to the buttons, but paused when Evie pulled a bottle of white wine out of the fridge.

"Uh, Evie? I don't think more wine is the answer right now."

"Actually, white wine can get out red wine, most of the time."

What? "But… but…"

"No, I swear it's true."

I shook my head in disbelief. "Why would anyone waste perfectly good wine that way?"

She laughed. "Right? Bra, too."

I looked down to see the stain on my favorite bra, as well. *Hmmm.*

"Don't worry, Dom won't be home for a while. If that's what you're worried about."

What *was* I worried about? Showing my friend my mosquito bite boobs? "Okay, okay," I said, then unhooked it and handed it over.

"Just gotta get something from the bathroom."

I stood there in the kitchen, bare from the waist up. My nipples tightened in the air, and I wrapped my arms around myself self-consciously.

Evie reappeared with a plastic bottle in her hand, rolling her eyes at me. "Why are you being so shy? I remember a night last year when you dressed me in your own underwear!"

She had a point. I could expose myself to Jake. Hell, even Dom had seen me with my pants down in the foyer. Why was I being weird about this? In the back of my head, I knew it was because I felt inadequate compared to Evie's lush curves. She was so… feminine.

"This is what I mean, Annie," my friend said pointedly. "Trust yourself and stop caring what other people think."

"Fine." I dropped my arms.

"There you go. Now get out some new glasses for the white." She pointed to a cabinet, then turned toward the sink with my clothes in hand.

"Evie, are you developing a drinking problem?"

"You're the one dribbling it on yourself."

I stepped over to stand beside her at the sink, curious about what she was using. I always struggled to get red wine out.

"Dish soap and hydrogen peroxide," she told me as she mixed them gently over the stains.

As I leaned forward, the cold granite of the countertop on my bare skin made my nipples tighten. Evie glanced over at me.

"Nice boobs, by the way."

It took everything in me *not* to cover myself at that moment. "Gee, thanks."

"I'm serious!"

I rolled my eyes. "Says Marilyn Monroe."

"Oh, for fuck's sakes." She dropped my shirt and bra in the sink with the sponge then stripped off her own shirt before I could stop her.

"Evie, what are you doing?"

"Proving a point. Look at me."

"I can't help it!"

Her breasts seemed bigger after she slipped off her bra. For some reason, I couldn't stop staring at them. It was like I was a teenage boy, unsure what to do with a naked woman, and I said as much to her.

"That's your problem. You keep thinking because you're not built like a porn star, you're not sexy. Do you know how jealous I am that you can wear any kind of clothes you want? They all look good on you."

I glanced down. "Um, I wish I had clothes on right now."

My friend made a huffing noise and lifted her heavy breasts up in her palms. "Touch them."

"What?"

"Come on, Evie, feel me up."

Was she joking? "Is there a camera hidden in here?"

"No, that's in the bedroom."

Somehow I doubted *that* was a joke. "You want me to what?"

"Touch. My. Tits!"

"Fine!" I squinted and jabbed my forefinger into a squishy part.

"*Ow!* That's not what I meant." She grabbed my wrist and clamped my palm to her breast. Held it there. "What does it feel like?"

I hesitated. Squeezed gently. "Soft?"

Her other hand whipped out and caressed one of my breasts before I could move. "So are yours," she told me.

My nipples perked instinctively at her touch. The sensation of her small, soft hand was weird, but not bad. When her thumb brushed over my nipple, I inhaled sharply.

Tentatively, my hands rose to cup her breasts more fully, stroking the sides with the tips of my fingers. Evie moaned, encouraging my curious touch. Investigating her warm curves was like an out-of-body experience, so accustomed was I to my own skin.

I half-laughed, half-sighed. "This is weird."

"See, Annie? You're sexy. Are you getting turned on at all by this?" Evie asked.

"Fuck, yeah."

We froze. Neither of us expected her question to be answered by Jake, who was standing by the couch.

JAKE

This was every guy's fantasy, right? Two beautiful women touching each other in front of me, oblivious to my arrival. It sure wasn't what I expected to find when I came to pick up Annie, but this was definitely not it.

I wasn't going to complain, however.

My arrival had gone unnoticed, while they giggled quietly. There was something irresistible about women laughing together. Men who didn't reflexively smile at it were either misogynists or so insecure that they immediately thought they were the joke.

Either way, they were fucking stupid.

I was anything but stupid, even if my brain felt a little fried after a day on the phone with buyers and suppliers. I'd been up half the night before, on the phone to China to sort out some manufacturing shit there. Dom did all the power lifting in his retail empire, and let me just have a few passion projects.

But even passion took work.

So, I was struck dumb when I walked in and saw

Evie's hands on Annie. It was Annie's gasp that took my dick from a shocked semi to a full, rock-hard, urge-to-rut erection.

I felt sudden sympathy for ancient ancestors who didn't know the science behind it all—only the overwhelming need to mate. That was how I felt right at that moment, like I could pull both women by their hair and compel them to their hands and knees.

I wanted to kneel behind them, spread them open, and fuck them until they were full of my seed. It was a primal instinct.

Evolutionary biology hadn't evolved all that much, I guessed. You could take a guy out of the cave…

"Yeah, I'm turned on," I drawled. "Looks like you two are, as well. Must have lost my party invitation in the mail."

Evie's eyes narrowed as I dropped my leather jacket over the back of the couch. Annie's gaze—which had yet to meet mine—went straight to my crotch as I adjusted myself in my dress pants. Then I unbuttoned the cuffs of my pale blue shirt, watching Annie carefully.

She'd admitted to me a few days before her weakness for "arm porn," as my girlfriend called it. Her breath had yet to even out as I rolled my sleeves up, exposing my tattoos. I *may* have flexed my wrists a little, just to mess with her.

Wait, my what? Girlfriend? I frowned and shook my head. Shit, that's not what I meant. My brain had gotten stuck on shuffle, in a playlist with only one song.

There were two girls here, and they were friends. That explained the brain fart.

Girl. Friend.

Evie winked at me, the little minx. "I was just telling Annie how sexy she is."

"Looks like you were demonstrating." I smirked at Evie's nonchalant shrug. Little virginal Evie had come a long way. "Should I leave you two alone?"

I was only half-kidding. No red-blooded hetero man would willingly walk away from this scene.

Evie hummed thoughtfully. "I don't know. Annie, what do you think?"

Annie made a strangled noise as she tried to become one with the kitchen island. I moved closer, standing over her, wanting her to look at me.

Needing her to look at me.

Despite all my primitive instincts to possess her, and all of Evie's joking aside, Annie's comfort meant… something to me. She was embarrassed; that much was obvious.

She was also—from the looks of it—*into it*. I had no problem with that, but I wasn't sure if she understood that it was okay.

"Annie."

I moved closer. Pushing back some of the silky hair falling around her face, I found her focused on my chin, color high in her cheeks. Unable to resist, I dipped down and kissed her.

When I pulled back and spoke again, my voice was rough. "Annie, look at me. Please."

Her head turned to Evie first, like she was asking permission? *Fuck that.*

"Honey, look at me." My voice was harder now.

She reluctantly met my gaze. Licked her lips. My pants tightened, but I kept my eyes on her. "It was the wine," she said, blushing.

I shook my head. "No, it wasn't."

Evie drifted down the hall to her bedroom, giving us some privacy.

Annie evaded my gaze again and moved to the sink. Picked up a sodden pile of clothes and dropped it again with a splat. "This isn't like me."

"It can be. You can be anything you want, Annie. I won't judge you." I'd done too much crazy shit in my time to be like that.

She tilted her head, looking confused.

"You want to hook up with Evie? I don't mind."

Her brown eyes widened, as round as the slightly almond shape of them would allow. "No! I mean, it just sort of hap—"

"Evie's right, you know," I interrupted. "You *are* sexy. You can blame the wine all you want, but maybe it's just you. You and Evie are both incredible, sensual, responsive women."

I looked up to see Evie eye me curiously as she put a t-shirt on the island. Annie cleared her throat, pulling my attention back to her.

"Both of us," Annie echoed, narrowing her eyes at me.

"Of course, both of you. My god, I want you all the fucking time. Understand?"

Her gaze flickered over my shoulder to where Evie stood. "Yeah. I think so." Her lips pressed together firmly, briefly. Then she exhaled, squeezing her eyes closed as though deep in thought.

Did she understand?

"You want to stay."

I rubbed at my forehead. "Sure, I want to stay a while. Unless you're ready to go home now?"

Wait, not home. Back to my place.

When she opened her eyes again, it was like she was looking right through me. *Annie had left the building.* I registered the strange blankness in her expression, but lost my train of thought as she pushed me aside.

Then she pushed her black pants down over her hips and kicked them off.

What was she doing?

"Uh, Annie…" Evie's voice was uneven behind me. "I brought you something to—"

"Why? We're sexy, remember? He wants us all the time." She looked at at me, her hips shifting in her red thong. It was like a flag to a bull.

I mean, it was *red*.

"You want us all the time, right?" she repeated.

And there was a wet spot. My mouth watered when I smelled her arousal.

I nodded. "Right." Slowly, carefully, I took her hand and pressed it to my crotch. "Feel that? That's what you do to me. All. The. Fucking. Time."

Annie raised an eyebrow. The blush that stained her cheeks traveled over her neck and down her chest again, like a path for my tongue to follow.

So I followed it.

She gasped when I tasted her heated skin, like a hot pan hissing with moisture. Steaming. Scalding. I made my way with an open mouth all the way over her chin to her mouth—which I took with hungry intent.

I groaned as she pulled away.

"Sexy," she said shakily, jerking her chin over her shoulder. "Right, Evie?"

A hum sounded in the distance. It could have been

Evie. It could have been the fucking fridge, for all I cared. All I saw was Annie.

Keeping her gaze on me, dark and guarded, she bent over a little to loop her fingers in the waistband of her thong. "Evie's sexy too, isn't she?" she asked me.

What? Was she she still in the room? "Yeah. Fuck, yeah." *Whatever.*

I'd been fighting this primitive urge to plunge into her tight, hot pussy since I entered the room. With very little grace, I dragged her panties down her legs, admiring the glistening streak left on her inner thighs.

While I was down there, I nuzzled the little tuft of dark hair at the juncture of her legs. *So sweet.*

"Need you." Her arousal clung to my tongue as I whispered. *More. I needed more.*

With a grunt, I buried my mouth in her, my hands clamping around her hips to steady her. My tongue curled inside her trembling core, savoring every drop of her desire. She jerked and twitched in my hold as I flattened my tongue and dragged it up her seam to the hard bud of her clit.

"Oh god, *Jake!*"

Her voice was an arrow, aimed straight at my cock.

"You want me to *prove* that you're sexy? That I want you?" I panted, pressing my forehead into the warm curve of her mound of Venus. Annie moaned softly as I circled her entrance with my fingertips.

How much more evidence did she need? I was eating her out in Dom and Evie's kitchen, for fuck's sakes.

"I just need to know... *ahhh...*" She trailed off as I reached deeper.

'Deeper' was never a goal of mine, but Annie sucked

me in—deeper into her body, deeper into her mind, deeper into her heart. But the deeper I went, the darker it got.

I was flying blind now, aroused beyond belief and losing track of our conversation. *How had this even started?* I was on my damn knees in front of her, and didn't know what more she wanted.

"What, honey? What do you need to know?"

Her thumbs slid over my cheekbones, tilting my head back to look up at her flushed face. "Do you want both of us?"

Both of—*what?* Annie *and* Evie, together? My lips parted as I struggled to understand, struggled for control. I was already close to exploding like a fucking teenager, and now this… offer?

She watched me carefully. "Wouldn't you like that, Jake? Wouldn't you like to fuck both of us?"

One of her thumbs lowered to tease the corner of my mouth. Without any hesitation, I drew it inside and sucked it hard against the roof of my mouth. Her hips twitched in response.

I still had one hand between her legs, her pussy pulsing around my fingers. "I want to fuck you," I told her. "I'm *going* to fuck you. In about ten seconds, I'm going to fold you over the goddamn counter and sink my dick into you."

"What are you waiting for?" She lifted an eyebrow and turned to the island.

And bent over.

"Uh, Jake?" Evie tried again to get my attention. *Yeah, good luck with that.*

Annie's slim body was plastered against the stone, her lower lips shiny with moisture and the shadow of her back entrance winking at me. She stretched further, the crease of her ass widening with the movement.

"Jacob Stone!" Evie's shouted.

"Ten seconds is up," Annie said, her face pink as she looked back at me. Gooseflesh rose on her pale backside.

Holy mother of fucking god. If I had thought Annie was a walking contradiction before, now she had me turned around and upside down.

In fact, those were two positions that I wouldn't mind trying with her.

Her face darkened as she taunted me. "Do it, Jake. Aren't you going to—*agh! Shit!*"

It took only a few seconds for me to undo my pants and free myself, and then I was deep inside her.

A primitive kind of roar burst from my chest as I drove home into that hot, sucking haven, my hips smacking the curve of her ass.

"Yeah! You wanted it? Now take it. *Take my cock.* I fucking burn for you, Annie, and I don't know what—other—proof—you—*need!*

She slapped her hands against the stone island as I slammed into her.

"Oh dear god."

In the back of my mind, I recognized that faint, stunned voice as Evie's.

In the front of my *body*, however, Annie's skin had begun blooming with marks left by my fingers and lips.

I dropped my head back briefly, dazed by the animal instincts driving me. My dick throbbed and my balls tightened—*no!* I didn't want to come this fast.

I wanted to claw at her hips until bruises appeared.

I wanted to fill her to overflowing, until my cum

dripped out of her—then spray her ass with my seed one more time to brand her skin as well as her soul.

If I could have crawled inside her at that moment, I would have. I'd never felt that kind of need to possess someone before.

"Is this the kind of proof you want?" I growled, admiring the way her pink flesh stretched around my dick as I thrust and withdrew. Mostly I thrust.

"Ungh!"

This… this 'demonstration' that she was sexy? That I wanted her? It was total bullshit, in a way. Her needs were secondary to mine at that moment. I'd devolved into a crude manifestation of sexual need.

Crude. Sexual. Need. That was pretty much it.

"Jake!" Annie's lips pursed, with her cheek smushed against the top of the island. Her eyes closed. "Evie," she panted.

What about her? I leaned over. "Evie what?"

My movements slowed to minute, intimate jerks against her as I molded my front to her sinuous and sweaty back. I was so goddamn close, in every way—yet I wanted to get *closer*. Still in a fog of hunger, I licked and sucked her shoulder and neck.

"Ev—" Annie tried again, twisting her head around to try to look me in the eye.

"Evie *what*?"

She yelped as I yanked her up to a standing position, and she reached out to grab the edge of the counter. After throwing me a dirty look over her shoulder, she looked straight ahead again before dropping her chin to her chest.

Tiny prickles of fire built in my balls, reminding me that I was close to the edge. Holding Annie like this brought me even closer. Her hair tickled my face as I plastered her against me, with one palm at her breast and the other splayed over her belly.

"Are you…?" She inhaled deeply, her hands covering mine over her expanding ribcage. "You going to fuck Evie, too?"

Shit, what?

At that moment, I lost any grasp I still had on my self-control. Pleasure shot through my body, and any ability to think and reason was sucked out of me in its wake.

"*Agh!* Fuck fuck *fuck!*" The tension in me uncoiled violently as I spurted helplessly into her—without a condom, *again*.

Apparently my brain cells were in my dick, and I was losing them at a rapid pace.

By the time I finished, I was trembling. My clothes were damp with sweat, with only my pants shoved down my hips, and Annie shivered—naked—in my arms.

Jesus Christ, had I even made her come? What kind of beast was I?

When I dropped my hands she leaned over the counter, trying to catch her breath.

"Must be something… about this… island," she murmured.

I looked down at my dripping cock and the moisture between her thighs. Then I frowned.

"Where's Evie?"

JAKE

"*J*ake, you are the dumbest motherfucker on the face of the earth."

I reared back as Dom laughed in my face. "Thanks, asshole."

Too late, I remembered that Stella was in the kitchen with Evie. Had she heard us? Glancing over, I saw that Evie and my daughter were deep in a cookie-making tutorial. Hopefully neither of them heard Dominic giving me shit.

It was a lazy Sunday afternoon, following a silent Sunday morning. After our nuclear encounter the night before, Annie retreated to a guest bedroom at Dom and Evie's and never came out. Evie gave me a dirty look, a raised eyebrow, and shoved me out the door.

My apartment was cold, quiet, and filled with my own restless energy for the rest of the night. Later in the morning, I picked up Stella from Sheila's.

It was going to be a sleepover night, since Sheila had a long shift that evening. She was still training in the dispatch job, and while the bags around her eyes were being packed for longer and longer trips, there was a satisfaction in them that I couldn't begrudge. The new job was agreeing with her, even if the scheduling sucked at times.

By the time Stella and I arrived at Dom and Evie's, Annie had already left for work. I was frustrated and annoyed at missing her, but when I grumbled to Dom about it, he just laughed.

And insulted my intelligence.

"Let me guess," I said. "Evie kissed and told."

He shook his head at me. "Well, yeah. It sounds like it was a pretty hot scene."

"Well, they were both topless and touching each other."

"No, I meant you bending Annie over the counter in front of Evie. Jesus, you have no boundaries, do you?"

"You desecrate the kitchen with Evie regularly," I pointed out.

"I live here!" Dom put down the newspaper he'd been reading on the couch and grinned at me. "But the girl on girl action sounded hot, too."

"Did it bother you?" For some reason my brain kept going to it, like a tongue seeking out a canker sore.

He waved his hand, making an indistinct sound in the back of his throat. "It is what it is. And like I said, it sounded pretty hot. I trust Evie. I don't think she's going to leave me for Annie, if that's what you're getting at."

I didn't know what I was getting at. But I felt like I'd been reaching in the dark since leaving their place less than twelve hours earlier.

"Okay, Mister Know-It-All. Why was Annie so…?"

"Adventurous?"

Well, that too. "Upset," I said.

Dom shook his head again, enunciating carefully. "Dumb. Mother. Fu—"

I put up my hand, jerking my head towards the girls in the kitchen. "Okay, I get it. I mean—I don't *really* get it."

With a frustrated huff, my adopted brother stood up from the couch, and I followed him to his home office. This room used to be a business sanctuary, but Evie's influence had crept in here as well—a new clock on the desk, a cushy chair by a bookcase.

"Sit down." He pointed to the armchair.

When I fell into the chair with a sigh, the midday sun shining through the window illuminated a swarm of dust motes.

Dom leaned against the desk, his arms crossed over his chest. "From what Evie told me… it sounded like a test."

"A test?" My mind raced, hurdling over the evening like a mental track and field competition. "I failed, didn't I?"

His dark eyebrows came together in an epic scowl. "Dude, you pooched it. Big time."

"What? What is it with women?" I groaned and pressed my fingers into my eyeballs. "How am I supposed to pass a test if I don't know I'm taking it? Obviously, I didn't even fucking study!"

"From what I heard, you did manage to get some cramming at the last minute."

I looked up. The bastard was smirking at me. "That's not funny."

"Bullshit. I'm hilarious. And you'd probably say something like it, too—if you were in my place."

Thinking back on the whole situation, I paused over

certain moments, then pressed play and paused again. Blinked and tried to do a mental screen capture. The problem was that my memory wasn't objective; it was biased toward my dick.

I blinked at Dom. "Is it because I got off before Annie did?"

"Did you get shot in the head in Iraq and just didn't tell anyone?" Dom huffed.

I didn't usually talk much about that time. I joined up because I wanted to belong to something without feeling like a pawn—as I had been since being adopted by Dominic's rich grandfather. He'd gone and plucked me out of foster care to be a playmate for his orphaned grandson, like we were living in some stupid Charles Dickens book.

Inevitably, I rebelled. So I busted my ass—and got it kicked on a regular basis—to become an elite soldier, so I wouldn't be a toy for entitled assholes to play with.

The joke was on me.

The military was one big role-playing game for politicians, most of whom didn't know the difference between a dungeon and a dragon.

"I'm not talking about Annie. Not really," Dom amended.

"Is it something about Evie?"

"You're getting warmer."

"Did I embarrass her?" She hadn't seemed too shy at the time, though I remember her saying my name a couple of times.

My adopted Richie Rich brother looked like he wanted to hit me. "Bag of rocks. You are as dumb as a—"

I threw up my hands. "Okay! Okay! Just spell it out, since I'm too fucking stupid to connect the dots, here."

"They thought you wanted a threesome."

My mouth opened, then closed. The thought had crossed my mind, but not seriously. It was just a floating fantasy, a male reflex. "But I never said—"

"You said we were both sexy," Evie reminded me from where she stood in the doorway to the home office.

I startled, looking behind her for Stella.

"She's playing in the living room with some kitchen stuff," she answered my silent question.

Kitchen stuff? "Like what?" I asked suspiciously.

"Just some knives, a cheese grater. A ninja blender thing." Evie lifted one shoulder.

Oh. She was joking.

"You *are* both sexy," I told her.

The corner of her mouth turned down. "You also said you wanted both of us."

"Well, yeah. At one time—separate times. Not together, right then." *Didn't I?* I rubbed my forehead.

"Then you proceeded to fuck Annie's brains out," Dom said.

Annie added, "While I left the room, like a lady."

"That's debatable," I muttered. If I recalled correctly, she'd left the show at intermission.

But yeah, after we'd—*I'd* finished, I'd wondered where she'd gone. I asked Annie where Evie—*oh. Oh, shit.*

"By George, I think he's got it," drawled Dom. Evie snorted, disappearing down the hallway again.

I dropped my head into my heads, groaning. "Fuck. My. Life."

"Looks like you're doing a pretty good job of that without help."

"Fuck you."

My brother sighed. "I get that maybe you didn't mean to, but it sounds like you made Annie think that you wanted Evie, as well. And Evie tells me that her friend is a little insecure about the whole fact that you've banged my fiancée before."

My forehead furrowed with a frown as I looked up at him. "You were there, too."

"Somehow, I don't think that fact fills Annie with confidence."

No, it probably didn't.

Annie was up and down, always unpredictable and at odds with herself. She was the kind of woman who would enter a hot dog eating contest just to prove that she wasn't a vegetarian.

"So what was I supposed to do?"

"Leave."

I jerked my head back in disbelief. "*Dude.* They were feeling each other up." My body began to react just at the memory.

Dom looked away uncomfortably. "Okay, fair enough. Shit, I don't know."

"What would you have done, in my place?"

Silence.

Right, I thought so.

"I gotta ask you, Jake. Do you still want Evie?"

"No! I mean, she's beautiful and sexy and everything, but I'm not in love with her." *Hadn't I said something like this to Annie?* "I never was. She's always been yours, even when I had her."

I met Dom's assessing gaze, wanting him to understand that I wasn't a threat to him or his relationship. I saw Evie as a sister. Okay, yes, a sister that I'd double-teamed with him at one point, but... She was just... Evie—soft, sassy, *real*.

In retrospect, I'd barely noticed her after seeing Annie's flushed face and pebbled nipples the night before.

All I saw was Annie.

All I *wanted* was Annie—the woman who didn't give a damn about my money or medals. The one who had no regard for her own personal safety, but looked at my little girl like she was made out of crystal.

"Okay, smart guy. What do I do now?" I asked him.

"Hang out, if you want. I think Evie's going shopping or something. Then take Stella and pick up Annie after the lunch service is done," he said, reminding me that there was no dinner at her restaurant on Sundays.

"I meant in a bigger picture kind of way."

Dom considered it. "Talk to her."

And say *what*?

ANNIE

I almost didn't expect Jake to come pick me up from work. When he did, I didn't know what to say to him. Luckily, I didn't have to say anything, as my manager John pulled him aside to talk about... something.

Whatever. I grabbed my stuff and said goodbye to the kitchen staff, who were still scrubbing things down. The dishwasher was broken, which left Darren steaming open his pores over a full sink of hot water. I felt bad for the guy.

"Do you want me to help?"

He shook his head, his face red. "I'll get the boss to pitch in."

I snorted. "Good luck with that." John was notoriously prissy. Then again, he might help out just to make sure it was done properly—not that Darren was a slacker. But there were a lot of brunch dishes there.

"Wow!" Stella had broken free of her father's gravity and wandered into the kitchen. "Can I have a peanut butter sammich?"

Everyone froze, unaccustomed to seeing a little kid in a commercial kitchen. I doubted we even had peanut butter.

"I'll make you one at home," I told her, scooping her up. "Say goodbye, Stella!"

"G'bye, Stella!"

"Sheesh." I rolled my eyes. "Do you practice being cute?"

She squirmed out of my arms and ran out into the front. The staff got back to work with fresh smiles on their faces. That kid was better than Prozac, sometimes. By the time I caught up with Stella, John was going through credit card receipts and Jake was waiting at the door.

"Ready?" he asked gruffly.

I nodded.

The walk back to Jake's apartment was quiet, except for Stella's shrieks as she swung like a monkey from his tattooed, muscled arm.

"Again!"

Yeah, kid. Again.

I envied her ability to hang on to Jake without a care, trusting that he would catch her if she fell. I'd never known a man like that. I certainly hadn't had a Daddy like that.

As a teenager, I spent some time trying not to get caught by my mother's asshole boyfriends. They seemed to think that jailbait was fair game if my mom was asleep. I got out of there as soon as I could, but my grades weren't good enough to get me very far.

Waitressing wasn't my dream job but it wasn't a nightmare, either. It was honest work and decent money, and until recently I'd been satisfied with it. Now I was almost thirty, and realizing that I'd been in my "temporary" job for nearly twelve years.

Shit.

It made me feel even worse for getting so comfortable at Jake's. I was a strong, independent, ninja woman! Okay, maybe not so much the ninja part.

I frowned and sighed. "You know…"

Jake nearly tripped when he heard me speak, swearing as he stumbled over Stella.

"Daaa-ddy!" Stella picked herself up from the sidewalk and gave us both a baleful look.

"Sorry, honey."

She stepped between us and took our hands. "Swing me!" she demanded as restitution.

Jake grinned at me over her head. Was that relief? Gratitude that I'd broken the awkward silence? Usually his smile did weird, wonderful things to my insides, but this one felt like I'd gorged on hot chocolate instead of tequila.

It took us a couple of tries to coordinate our arms, but soon Stella was swooping up and down like a tote bag on a really successful shopping trip.

"I know what?" Jake asked.

"What do you know?"

"You started to say something. 'You know…'"

I blinked. "Oh, yeah. My, uh, secret admirer seems to have given up. No notes, no presents, nothing."

He stopped, breaking his daughter's grip on him. "So you think he's forgotten about you? Stella, stop whining."

"I just think maybe I could go back to my own apartment."

Try to live my own life again. Get back to the place where I wasn't depending on other people to keep me safe and happy. Maybe I wouldn't have as much, but I wouldn't lose as much, either.

Stella tugged on my hand, trying to wrestle a swing out of me from sheer momentum. "Let's go!"

"Just a minute, starlight. We're almost home, anyhow." I looked at the sidewalk. "I mean—I'm sure you're wasting money on me…"

Jake stepped toward me, taking my other hand. The three of us stood in a circle, Stella yanking on us both and our free hands in each other's. We looked ready to have a séance, summoning spirits from beyond the grave.

He leaned in close, his voice harsh in my ear. "I don't know what's worse—the way you undervalue yourself, or the way you underestimate other people."

A hole opened up in my chest. "Like you?"

"Like me." His hand squeezed mine, completely surrounding it with warmth and strength. His daughter still held my other hand like I was a puppy on a leash. "And like *him*. You don't know what's capable of. You don't even know who he *is*, remember? Maybe he's just lulled you into a… what's the—?"

"False sense of security," I finished. *Yeah, I was familiar with the concept. It seemed to be the story of my life.* "I'm a big girl, Jake. I know how to dial nine-one-one, all by myself."

His eyes narrowed. "Okay, smart ass. Prove it."

Then he said nothing more while we walked the last block to his apartment.

Prove it? I didn't understand. "What, you want me to show you my phone or something?"

"Not exactly," he said. Once in the lobby, he gave

Stella his phone to play on and told her to go sit on one of the couches. I watched, confused, as he then spoke quietly to the security guard.

"Aren't we going upstairs?"

"Not yet." He unbuckled his belt as he stalked toward me, whipping it out of the loops on his pants with a swish. "Turn around."

"What?" Was he going to take his clothes off in the *lobby*?

Impatiently, he spun me around and pulled my hands back. My shoulder blades squeezed together. "Ow!"

"Sorry." He landed a soft, slow kiss on the nape of my neck. "Sorry, sorry, sorry." Each apology came with the press of his lips, the tip of his tongue, the heat of his breath. It all rendered me to a liquid form, relaxing me into that sweet, mellow complacency we talked about.

Until he wrapped his belt around my crossed wrists.

What the—?

The leather squeaked a little as he pulled my makeshift binding as tight as possible. My gaze flew to the guard, who was looking down at his phone. Even Stella was immersed in Jake's phone.

"Jake, I don't think—"

He stepped in front of me to silence my protest with his mouth.

Damn, he was too good at that.

Then he fished my phone out of my pocket and placed it in the pot of one of the artificial *ficus* trees dotting the lobby, before flopping down on the couch beside Stella.

"Now, call." He raised his arms to lace his fingers behind his head. Smug.

My mouth fell open. "What?"

"Come on, Annie. This should be easy. Your legs are free, you're not shot up with sedatives or heroin, you know where you are, and you can identify your assailant. You have lots of information to give the dispatcher. This is really the best case scenario."

I shook my head. "You're crazy."

Yes, operator, I'm being held hostage by my boyfriend while his daughter plays Angry Birds. What's he doing, you ask? Teaching basic physics, it seems. And smirking.

There were times that Jacob Stone's smirk was kryptonite for my panties.

This was not one of those times.

"Okay, fine." *I could do this.*

"I could have tied you to a chair," he reminded me as I walked over to the potted plant. "Or hog-tied you."

I stared at him. "Uh, thanks?"

His eyes twinkling with mischief, he mouthed "sexy" at me.

Okay, I just had to get the phone out of the planter. No problem. But my hands were behind me, so I turned my back on the ficus and tried to squat and lean backward at the same time. My fingertips brushed against the leaves. I lowered further, like I was doing a limbo game at a party.

And lost my balance.

I pulled against the belt handcuffs with the compulsion to windmill my arms out, my shoulders feeling the tension. In my effort not to plant my ass in the pot along with the ficus, I overcompensated and fell forward.

My knees slammed into the floor. My face followed.

"Shit!" Jake launched himself off the couch and to

the floor beside me. "I'm sorry, maybe that was a bad idea. Are you okay?"

Pain throbbed in my legs, and my neck ached from the effort of avoiding full facial contact with the floor. I turned my head to the side and rested it on the cold, dirty tile.

"Yeah, I'm just great. My boobs broke my fall." *Barely.*

He bit back a chuckle. "Are *they* okay?"

"Don't you dare feel me up for broken bones right now, Stone." Wriggling like a fish out of water, I tried to get back on my knees. *Bad idea. Ouch!* "Motherfu—!"

Jake's hand slapped over my mouth and he jerked his head toward Stella. When he removed it, I glared at him.

"I don't see you putting any money in the swear jar, mister."

He shrugged. "I'm her father. She's hard-wired to ignore me."

I managed to roll onto my side, dust coating my black shirt and pants. "You gonna untie me, here?"

"Nope. You still haven't called for help."

"Help! Help!"

The security guard was useless, instead shepherding people around us between the street and the elevators. The rubberneckers probably thought we were doing some weird improv thing, or shooting a video.

"With your phone, ninja girl." Jake sighed as I bent my knees and started spinning in a circle on the floor, trying to get a foot underneath myself. "Okay, hang on."

I'd just managed to get myself to an almost sitting position, my legs bent to the left behind me, when he put my phone on the floor in front of me.

"Really?" I asked.

"Go ahead," he said, settling back down on the couch six feet away. "Call nine-one-one."

I spun around, reaching for the phone with my hands still behind my back. What followed was possibly the most awkward, humiliating, futile experience of my entire life—and I'm including losing my virginity to the Mathletes captain in my senior year.

It would have helped to *see* the buttons on the face of my smartphone when entering my passcode.

Bzzz.

Bzzz.

Bzzz.

I was at serious risk of disabling the damn thing. With a huff, I wriggled back around on my ass to face the phone. It sat there on the floor, taunting me.

Jake sat on the couch, taunting me.

Stella snuggled under his arm, engrossed in pigs taunting birds. *Birds...* that gave me an idea.

With as much control as I could muster—and that wasn't a whole lot—I bent at the waist like a lever. My face was so close to the phone that my breath fogged up the screen.

Yes!

No.

No, it turned out that one's nose did not equal a thumbprint ID. Nor was it that great for the passcode. It might have worked for facial recognition, but I wasn't sure I would recognize me at that moment, much less the phone.

"Miss Annie?"

My chin jerked up at Stella's little voice. My ponytail was falling out, my hair a wispy cloud around my face that I had to blow away in order to see the frown on her face.

"Whatcha doing?"

Good question. Leave it to a three year-old to point out the absurdity in my current situation. I was sitting on the floor in the lobby of a ritzy condo building, looking like a cat burglar that had just been caught in a citizen's arrest.

My whole body caved in. "Okay, Jake. You win."

ANNIE

*J*ake waited until Stella was tucked away in her princess bed and I was relaxing in a hot shower before he ambushed me.

"So, about that thing yesterday…"

His voice startled me as much as his presence—hot, hard and naked behind me. When I jerked my head back in surprise, I knocked his chin. He swore, his hands flying to my upper arms.

"Did you do that on purpose, ninja girl?"

"Why would I do that?" It hurt the back of my head and got water in my eyes.

He turned me around slowly, pulling me out of the water enough to face me directly without the spray between us. "To get me back for earlier?"

"You're going to have to be more specific."

Did he mean the bondage game in the lobby?

Did he mean the aborted threesome the night before?

The dinosaur chicken nuggets he overcooked for dinner?

He tilted my chin up to look me in the eye. I didn't even have the excuse of the water in my face to avoid him.

"Last night, with Ev—last night. I owe you an apology." Shame clouded his eyes, along with the steam.

"For?"

His hands and gaze moved over my body, like he was looking for something. Or memorizing me? "For being so rough. For confusing you."

My mouth went dry, despite the moisture around us. "What are you saying?" *That he regretted it?* My stomach flipped at the possibility. The dino-dinner didn't help.

"I acted like a fucking caveman."

"I didn't mind," I said. And I hadn't, not that part.

It was unbearably hot, the way he just… took me. If he'd been someone else, I probably would have felt powerless. The fact that I felt so safe with Jake, though, made his aggression less frightening.

The only part I'd struggled with was my jealousy, and the fear that he also wanted—

"*Evie…*" I mumbled, looking down.

Jake grunted, closing in on me until his half-hard cock nudged my hip, his hands heavy on my shoulders.

"Annie. Annie, honey, look at me."

I took in the hard planes of his stomach and the muscles in his chest. A scar here and there. The change in skin tone on his upper arms, like a permanent farmer's tan.

Focusing on Jake Stone's body wasn't a hard thing to do. It was a privilege, like admiring an ancient sculpture.

Meeting his gaze directly again was more difficult, but I did it—even if I blinked like the loser of a staring contest.

He sighed. "Good girl. Keep looking at me, okay? I need you to hear this, and I get the feeling that your heart is deaf or something when you're not looking in my eyes."

Oh. How was it possible to shiver like this while standing under hot water?

There was so much truth in the lines around his eyes and mouth, in the frown on his forehead... that I couldn't move if I tried.

My chest was tight, but he held me tighter.

"Are you listening to me, ninja girl?"

I nodded.

"I don't want Evie. Evie is a..." He broke off, tipping his head back as though there might be a script to follow on the ceiling. "Great woman. She's a great woman," he repeated, before meeting my gaze again. "But she's Dom's woman. He's going to marry her. End of story."

"But—"

"She could take off her clothes and jump on my dick and I would look her in the eye and tell her to get the fuck off."

Yeah, right. "But—"

His thumb pressed over my lips. "No buts. Maybe you heard what you wanted to hear, or I didn't say it right. But last night I wanted you—I always want *you.* You've had my eyes crossed since you attacked me outside your building."

I swallowed around the lump in my throat. "That might have been my fist in your windpipe. Maybe I gave you some brain damage." It would explain a lot.

"You're a riot. No, I let my dick do all the thinking last night."

Reflexively, I looked down at his big, fat… brain.

Jake wrapped his arms around my waist, pulling me so close I could only feel him throbbing against me as my hands came up to rest against his chest. The shower spray beat down on my neck. Needles of heat tattooed my spine, until the water flowed over his hands at the lower curve of my back.

"Annie."

Right. Eye contact. My breath caught in my throat at the fierce expression on his face.

"The last woman I trusted gave me a daughter, and it didn't work out." He exhaled, pressing his forehead to mine. "Now, leaving aside the questionable intelligence of my dick… I want to trust *you*. Will you give me something in return?"

I gulped. "If you say you want a son…"

My mouth was faster than my brain, as usual. It was easier to joke than to take him seriously. Easier not to get hurt.

His head rose, a blinding grin cracking his serious expression. "No, honey. I want you to trust me. To give me a *chance*."

"A chance," I echoed.

"Stop holding the past against me. Stop running away from me. Stop fucking fighting me on everything."

I searched his face. All I saw was honesty and stubborn intent. If I didn't give Jake Stone the chance he wanted, he might just take it anyhow. The truth was that after all this time—this intense, push-pull, instant family, in-each-other's-faces time—he'd earned that chance.

"I don't—"

"Jesus, woman!" he groaned. "You're arguing with me now!"

I shook my head. "No, I'm——" Wait, I was. Why was my automatic response to disagree with him, when inside I really didn't?

With a deep breath I spread my fingers on his chest, to reach as much of him as possible. The strong, steady beats of his heart pulsed against my palm. I turned my face up to his, meeting his gaze as openly and honestly as I could.

"I don't want to fight anymore."

"Really?"

I nodded. I could almost see him thinking: *Is she telling the truth? Was she fighting with me or against me? Did it really matter?*

Whatever he saw in my face answered his questions, so I would no longer question his answers.

His mouth covered mine with a deep, possessive kiss. It stole any fear I held onto, and when he pulled back I was breathless.

"Wait." Reaching behind me, he turned off the water.

The sound of our breathing seemed even louder when no longer muffled by the shower. His handprint smeared across the fogged glass as he felt for the door and opened it.

Inch by inch, he shuffled me across the en suite bathroom and toward his bed. He held me close, like we were magnets drawn together.

My hair was still drenched, water dripping down my back and over my ass. Jake seemed to be able to shake it all off like a dog. We fell onto the bed, caring only that it was a soft place to land.

He branded me with his lips——on my mouth, cheeks, neck, collarbone, forehead. I tensed we lay on our sides, facing each other. If his passion collided with mine, it could be too hard, too fast. Instead, he slowed down and drew back to look at me.

I didn't think about the danger of loving him.

All I knew was that with Jake, my hollow spots were all filled.

I let out the breath trapped in my chest in a shaky hum. Then I leaned forward and kissed him. His body vibrated under my hands, struggling to contain his desire. My hands paved a path up and down his back as I opened my mouth to him. There was no hesitation, no pause before he swept his tongue into my mouth.

The empty space between us slid sideways and wavered, like a rip in the space-time continuum. The room around us swallowed all sound, the world beyond the apartment shrinking. My entire universe had collapsed on itself, compressing into the white-hot points of contact between our bodies.

What on earth could possibly come next? I wondered.

The problem with comparing intimacy and desire to the universe is that the latter is inexpressibly infinite. How did you compete with that? No matter how bad the odds, however, I knew Jake would try.

We took our time, learning each other through touch and taste and smell. For maybe the first time, I felt as though he'd been able to crawl inside my skin and feel what it was like to be me, and vice versa.

When he finally moved between my legs and entered me, I embraced him fully. For all his earlier demands, though, his fingers and tongue and cock inside me stroked, not plunged. The gentleman inside him still gave me an out, even if he didn't know it.

"Give me more," I begged him.

He took my face in his hands as he throbbed deep inside me. "Annie, I'm giving you everything I can. Don't you know that?"

His words penetrated me deeply, filling me with pleasure so intense that it made my heart hurt.

"It's not like before," I gasped. "Before... before, we were..."

"Fucking." The way he growled it made me hotter as his hips moved and he swelled within me.

I nodded.

Jake's chest pressed against mine as he took a deep breath. "That was before, honey. This——"

When he paused, my throat became tight with fear at what he would say. What did I want him to say? We were both afraid of a real relationship, but this... thing between us no longer felt like simple lust. If lust was ever simple.

Then he kissed me, slowly and gently, like a prince in a fairy tale. Bringing me to life again. His eyes were dark and shining when he raised his head.

"Annie, this is *after*."

It wasn't a false promise. He wasn't placating me. It came from his heart. When I closed my eyes, tears slid down my overheated cheeks.

He stilled. "Am I hurting you?"

I shook my head. "Not yet."

His sigh enveloped me. "Feel me, Annie." His hips moved lazily against me, but I felt him more inside my brain than my body.

"I'm full of you," I groaned.

He sped up his pace, his jaw tight. With one hand, he reached down and wedged his hand between us.

"You feel that?" he asked, his fingers moving between my clit and where he entered me.

"Oh my god." I felt it *all*.

My head tilted back, my orgasm swelling within me. When it came, it was in waves that nearly choked me and pulled me under. He held onto me tightly, burying his face in my neck.

"Oh fuck, Annie." His voice was hoarse as he jerked and twitched, grunting softly into my hair.

This was the scary part.

This was the blissful part.

This was the *after*.

JAKE

*D*om asked me once what it was like to be a parent. At the time, I wasn't seeing Stella enough, and think I said something bitter, like "fuck if I know."

But it was… relentless.

Relentless in the way that desert sand gets in every crack, crevice and pore of your clothes and body. Relentless, like how self-doubt, fear and guilt can plague your subconscious.

And that was just during the waking hours.

Even relentlessness had a routine, however. Within a few weeks, the three of us had found a rhythm. Well, as much as possible with Stella going back and forth between her mom's and my place.

That was the point of the conversation I had just started with Sheila.

"Is your schedule going to be regular soon?" I asked her. I dropped Stella's little *Frozen* backpack inside the front door of her apartment.

"I hope so. I think so." Sheila looked tired, but

also… happy? "I really like this job, so I'm praying the hours don't kill me. I feel like I'm making a difference, and god knows it's never boring."

I understood what she meant, but I also understood the toll it could take on a person. I was a complete asshole to almost everyone for close to six months after I finished my last tour.

There was no point in reminding her that she didn't *need* this job, given what I contributed to her and Stella's bank accounts. Honestly, I was impressed by her initiative. My bitterness of the last couple of years was easing.

Maybe Annie was right, and she had given me brain damage.

"Who's Annie?" Sheila asked. "Stella talks about her."

She'd opened Stella's backpack and was looking inside, her tone carefully casual. I wasn't stupid. She was fishing, and not just inside the backpack.

What to tell an old girlfriend about a new one?

"She's, uh, staying with me."

"Houseguest?" Her tone was sharper now. *Was that jealousy?*

I rubbed my neck, not sure how to label it. *Hostage, houseguest, hookup… heart?* "Sort of. Sort of not."

She tossed the backpack onto the couch, her voice hard. "I don't want Stella around some casual—"

"Watch it…"

Sheila's hands went to her hips. "Fine. Fling. Whatever. I won't have her exposed to that."

"Exposed to what, exactly? A nice woman who knows how to pour her a bowl of cereal?" *And makes bacon, while knowing all the words to Stella's favorite songs? The horror!*

I crossed my arms over my chest, my legs unconsciously spreading out into a ready-for-combat stance. Sheila was such a hypocrite. She seemed to have forgotten what kind of casual fling *she'd* exposed *me* to.

"Go ahead. Tell me exactly what kind of woman you think I'm exposing our daughter to."

I waited for the snide, passive aggressive insults; the paranoid fear that our little girl was going to be emotionally scarred by spending time with another woman who wasn't her mother or her mother's mother. Or Evie. Or a preschool teacher. Seriously, she was around other women all the time.

Sheila had always been a bit... what was the word? Helicopter-y? I immediately bristled when I saw her blades starting to spin, her mind whirling with assumptions and judgment. She bit her lip, sighed, and the *voop voop* slowed down to a dull whine.

"Okay. Sorry. I'll give you—and her—the benefit of the doubt."

My eyes widened. This was definitely progress. We exchanged a tired smile. "Look at us," I said. "Being grown-ups."

"It's probably about time. In a couple of years Stella will be more emotionally mature than you."

And *there* was the snide insult. It was almost a relief. There was only so much personal growth I could manage in a month.

~

*W*ithout Stella to plan around and Annie at work, I went to the office and worked through dinner. It wasn't the first time, nor would it be the last. I didn't even bother ordering food in, but raided the granola bars in the staff kitchen.

"Corporate MREs, Dominic. Look into it," I'd suggested at one meeting. *"It could be huge."*

At the moment I was immersed in researching possible locations for expanding the Stella toy store. Part of me didn't want to create another one. It was one of a kind, just like its namesake.

My passion project.

The business part of me, though, knew that it would be a good idea. It was hard enough to be a big retail empire and appear to have a heart and conscience these days. Stella would expand the Stone brand and position it in a positive way.

I hadn't realized how late it was until I saw the darkness outside the window, and my eyes were burning from staring at the computer screen.

Even with my fists pressed against my closed eyes, I noticed when the lights in the room went on.

"You *are* still here." Dom looked just as meticulous and fresh as when I saw him earlier. Only the dark shadow on his jaw indicated that time had passed.

I, on the other hand, didn't even bother with a suit jacket. What the fuck was the point?

"You want to go get a late dinner? Evie's hungry."

"Now? That's a really late dinner." Although, there was no reason *not* to, and I could eat.

"She's always hungry."

"Wedding stress getting to her?"

"More like my *big billionaire dick* getting to her," he joked. "I knocked her up."

"Dude! Seriously?"

Dom looked ridiculously pleased with himself. "It's early, but yeah."

Something flared through me, an emotion I couldn't pinpoint. Maybe it was just surprise, or recognition that their lives would change.

"How early?" I asked.

I hesitated to congratulate him, recalling a sad, scotch-soaked scene from the fall. Evie had lost a pregnancy at ten weeks, and it had hit them hard. Hopefully Dominic hadn't just jinxed it by telling me.

"Really early, but I just had to tell you. You know the way they calculate that shit is stupid, right? It should just be counted from the date my guys hit the target."

"Congratulations, I guess. She okay?"

"Other than puking in the morning—so far, so good."

"I'd throw up if I woke up to you, too."

He gave me the finger. "So, you guys want to have dinner?"

"Sure." It was embarrassing how many things in my body popped as I stood up. *How long had I been sitting there? Jesus.* I rolled the sleeves of my shirt down. "Are the girls ready?"

"We still have to pick Annie up, right?"

I froze in the middle of plucking my leather jacket off the back of the stiff little love seat in the corner of my office. "Stiff," because I knew from experience it was uncomfortable as fuck to sleep on.

"What are you talking about? Evie was supposed to pick Annie up after she dropped Stella at Sheila's."

It wasn't ideal, but it was the best we could organize. It had been a clusterfuck of a day, with meetings that wouldn't end and trying to juggle big and little people's schedules.

"They told me she went home early," Evie said as she walked through my office door. "Just call her."

Irritation flared in me. Why hadn't she texted me? Why had she left work? Was she sick? Injured? She'd told me about some of the gory accidents that could happen in a restaurant kitchen, and my mind immediately went to the emergency room.

I grabbed my phone off the corner of the desk and thumbed out a quick message to her. Then another. Waited thirty-three seconds, then sent another.

"Jesus, man. Give her a chance to respond."

Sticky tendrils of tension spun a web between the three of us as we waited for my phone to buzz or beep. *Something*. The gurgling of Evie's stomach was the only sound in the room.

"Sorry," she whispered. "Try calling her. I don't know why people always text first, every time. I mean, it's a *phone*."

It went straight to voicemail—twice.

"Shit."

"It's okay." Evie patted my arm. "Why don't we just go back to your place and pick up dinner on the way? Maybe she's sleeping or something."

I sure hoped so.

ANNIE

"Mmmm." I snuggled into my pillow, my eyelids weighed down by sleep and still feeling swollen and gritty.

Oh god, that felt so good. There was nothing like your own pillow. The cool side always felt cooler, and the warm side smelled like your own skin and shampoo.

Actually, that was a little creepy.

I nuzzled the pillowcase anyhow, luxuriating in the comfort it gave me. Then I paused. It smelled… weird. Not like "dance club odor on your hair after going out" smells, but… laundry soap or fabric softener. Something about it teased at my brain.

What kind of detergent was it? I flashed on the memory of doing Jake and Stella's laundry—along with my own, of course. Nothing said co-habitation more than washing someone else's dirty underwear. Of course, Stella was still struggling with potty training; I'd discovered that the hard way.

I'd discovered a lot of things the hard way in the previous twenty-four hours. My head still throbbed, and

I kept my eyes closed and ran through the day before like clips from a bad movie.

After lunch, Jake had gotten sucked into a conference call about china suppliers—the toy tea sets, not the country—and marooned Stella and I. I'd already helped her change her clothes twice in the morning, and had become an eagle-eye expert on identifying her "pee pee dance."

When it became clear that I was going to be late for my shift, Jake prompted me to call Dominic on another phone and ask him for an escort. To say I was irked was an understatement. For god's sakes, it had been close to a month! Was I going to be babysat like Stella indefinitely?

But that begged another question: what to do with Stella?

I didn't know that much about little kids, but I was pretty sure that three year-olds were supposed to be supervised. This three year-old's father didn't appear to be wrapping up his meeting anytime soon.

When Dom arrived, Stella was doing her second lap around the living room without touching the floor. I'd been "supervising," naturally.

"Nice parkour, kid."

"Uncle Dumb!"

She squealed and launched herself at him from atop the end table. I dove for the juice box that she'd kicked over in her welcome. Thankfully it was empty.

"Uncle Dumb?" I hadn't heard that one before. My giggles ended as soon as one mutated into a snort.

"*Dom* was hard for her to say at first. I'm sure she'll figure it out at some point."

"Hopefully after she's eighteen," I muttered.

"Stella, get off me. Isn't he done yet?" he asked, peeling his niece off his chest and jerking his chin toward Jake's den slash home office.

Stella vaulted onto the couch again, her curls bouncing around her face. No doubt—kids were cute, but they were hell on the furniture.

"I wanna come with you!" she announced, but it was unclear which "you" she meant.

"I'd better ask him."

Different voices collided in the den. Clearly his conference wasn't even close to finishing. Not wanting to interrupt him, I tapped him on the shoulder. He spun around in his chair, away from his computer, eyebrows raised.

"So you're saying that we need to find a different source for the pattern printing? It's just transferware." he asked. I looked at him blankly, until I realized he was addressing his colleagues.

I improvised some sign and body language to communicate: *"I'm going to work. What about Stella?"*

Laughter echoed from a speaker.

He whipped his head around. "Just a minute," he said to the computer—the screen with people's faces on it.

Oh my god. I'd been in full view of the webcam, miming a preschooler's pee pee dance. Mortified, I darted to the side, out of the way of the webcam. In my zeal to escape, I bounced off a wall.

More laughter.

Clearly I'd been wrong about the camera's field of vision.

At that point I just slunk out of the room. When I

got back to the living room, I found a red-faced Stella and Dom with his face twisted into a grimace.

"She peed on me."

"I'm sorry!" she wailed.

Her bow-legged cowboy walk of shame to the bathroom might have been amusing if it didn't mean another mess to clean up. I sighed. It was my fault; too many juice boxes, and no "pee pee dance" tutorial for Uncle Dumb.

A third change of clothes later for Stella, I was now officially late for work. What was the plan? I couldn't exactly take the kid to work with me.

Blissfully ignorant of the drama outside his den, Jake popped his head out to ask Dom if Evie was home today. Within a minute, it was all arranged that Stella would go to Dom and Evie's for a few hours. No miming required, except for the X-rated gesture he gave me in silent promise for later that evening.

Since he hadn't been the one cleaning up urine all morning, I offered him a different kind of hand gesture.

The rest of the day was equally pissy. I went over it all in my mind, hoping against hope that if I kept my eyes shut, it would turn out to just be a dream. I wanted to put my head under the covers and not come out.

My manager was close to losing his shit when I rushed in. I was annoyed as hell at being late—and made even later by having to move Stella's car seat to Dominic's sleek sedan. If Jake hadn't been so overprotective, I could have just gone to work by myself and Dom could have waited with Stella until Jake was done his meeting.

Instead, everybody had to be moved around like

pawns on a chessboard. And everything was so black and white.

I started my shift almost snarling with irritation.

Dom's patronizing reminder that Evie would pick me up later didn't help. I waved him off, feeling like a surly teenager. *Blah blah blah. Thanks, Dad. Can I have twenty bucks?* Only Stella blowing me a kiss from the back seat lifted my grumpy mood—and only a little.

It had been a long, shitty shift, and it wasn't even eight o'clock. I was in the weeds all evening, distracted and grumpy. For a professional waitress, I sure wasn't acting very professional—and it showed.

"What is going on with you tonight, Annie?" my manager asked me as I sucked back a Diet Coke by the bar. "Boy trouble?"

I pasted my second-best "customer service smile" on my face. I didn't have enough energy to dole out my best smile. "Boys? What are boys?" I blinked at him. "I live for my job, John."

He snorted. "Yeah, I've seen the boys you've been hanging out with lately. I'm surprised you still have a job, but I guess they have to let you out of bed sometime."

I gaped at him. Had I heard him right, or had the constant background noise screwed with my ears? "I'm sorry?" My boss had never spoken to me like that before.

Another server came up to us with panic on her face. I recognized the expression. So did my manager, who just sneered at me before steering her away to discuss whatever new catastrophe had occurred.

The clinking of dishes and hum of conversation floated around me as I replayed John's snide comments.

Was he insinuating that I was sleeping with both Jake and Dom? If so, did he mean together, or at the same time? My stomach churned. *Jesus Christ, what kind of impression was I giving people?*

And had he threatened my job, because of it?

For the next half an hour, I was so distracted that I couldn't even muster up my fifth-best customer service smile. John's words echoed in my head, and I waited for the panic over potentially losing my job to paralyze me.

It didn't.

Huh.

"Get it together, Annie!" John muttered at me when I brought back the second order I'd screwed up. One of the line guys scowled at me as he ripped the revised ticket from my hand.

John grabbed my arm. "Do you need to go home early?"

It sounded less like a compassionate suggestion and more like a parental threat to a misbehaving kid. My hackles went up, but I bit my tongue.

"No. I'm sorry." I reddened, my face heating as I waited by the pass.

If I was stuck in a holding pattern, it might be good for me to break out of it. Right?

Without my realizing it, Jake had given me a safety net, psychologically and otherwise. After years of taking care of myself, I now found myself in a strange new family dynamic with Jake and Stella—and I liked it.

The new plate slid under the warmer, and I grabbed it. When I looked down at the pasta, my first thought wasn't relief that the order got fixed—it was "Stella would love this."

"Annie!"

I'd tipped the plate sideways in my shock. "Sorry!" I righted it and used a clean cloth to wipe the side.

The guys would almost certainly be pissed off that I'd ruined their careful plating, but I couldn't care less as I walked like a zombie out of the kitchen and into the dining room.

Oh my god.

I was in love with Jake.

With Jake and Stella.

Now I dropped the plate.

Logically, I knew that not every single person in the restaurant stopped their meals and conversations to stare at me—but it sure felt that way.

With my nose prickling, I tried to take a deep breath, but my chest squeezed painfully. My vision was blurry with the threat of tears as I fell to my knees to clean up.

"Annie!"

John squatted beside me, his face as red as mine felt —only his didn't have big, hot tears rolling down it.

"I'm sorry," I said dully. "I'll fix it."

"You're kneeling in the sauce."

"I'm sorry."

"You need to go home," he said softly.

With shaking hands, I tried to pick up it all up. The pasta slipped through my fingers. "It's okay, I can—*ah!*" I hissed as the sharp edge of the broken plate slid over my thumb.

John swore. It didn't look good to have the staff bleeding on the food. "Go to my office," he ordered.

There was a lull in the ambient noise as I rose to my feet and plodded to the back. When I put out my hand to avoid running into a wall, I left an *alfredo* handprint.

Dammit, why was I still crying? I felt like something had

burst inside me, and I couldn't contain the flood of intense emotions.

Love.

Fear.

Confusion.

They came and came and came, washing over me until I was exhausted.

Even now, lying on my stomach and burying my head under my pillow like an ostrich, I felt drained.

And it still smelled odd. It niggled at my brain. *What was it?*

Pulling my head out, I propped myself up on my elbows to sniff the pillowcase. My hands curved over the bump of the neck support inside the pillow, squeezing the foam and feeling it rebound like a marshmallow under my fingers.

I opened my eyes, recognition penetrating my brain.

This was *my* pillow.

Mine. Not Jake's.

I was in *my apartment*. And I wasn't alone.

"Good, you're awake. I knew that gown would suit you."

ANNIE

I felt like I'd just plunged through the icy crust of a winter pond. Dark. Cold. Suffocating. Swirling around me.

Slowly, I looked down and saw the gaping neckline of the white satin gown, like snow drifting over my body. It was all I wore; the fancy bridal lingerie was missing.

But then so were the bra, panties, and clothes I wore to work.

Shit fuck damn.

Instinctively I wriggled down under the blanket.

"Awww, don't do that. You'll wrinkle it. I spent a lot of money on that outfit."

I froze as John stood up from the couch and stalked over to me. *Think, Annie, think!* "Um, thanks for bringing me home, but…" I bit my lip, unsure what to say.

My head spun like a top skimming over everything —the notes that came to me at work, the flowers, the chocolate.

Fast forward to the accident at work.

Going into John's office, covered in pasta sauce and

humiliation. He brought me something to drink and bandaged the cut on my thumb while I began to calm down. Then he said I should go home.

I remembered his hand on my lower back as he walked through the restaurant with me. I remembered being out on the street with him. I remembered stumbling.

But then that was it—until now, as he stood over me with a strange smile on his face.

"Oh, that's right. You don't live here anymore, do you?" He shrugged nonchalantly, but his hands curled into tight fists at his sides. "My bad."

"What? No, I still live here!" *Didn't I? Technically.*

His knuckles were turning white. "You've been whoring yourself out to the Stone brothers."

The sarcastic phrase "Well, that escalated quickly" came into my head and I shook it right off. This was not the time for a pithy remark. I needed to defuse this situation.

"No, no. Remember Evie, John? She's engaged to one of them. I've been helping them with the wedding planning."

Yeah, the wedding that I'd managed to completely put out of my mind. The one that—a million years ago—Jake had proposed attending together.

I laughed weakly. "You really got the wrong impression. It's kind of funny when you think about it."

My manager didn't look amused. Or convinced that he was wrong.

"Don't lie to me, Annie. One of them talked to me about your 'stalker.'" He sneered as he made air quotes.

Think. Think! "Not a stalker! He found out that I had

a secret admirer. Maybe I bragged to Evie; I was so flattered…"

John shook his head. "No, he said you were scared. Why were you scared?" He reached out to peel down the top of the blanket.

I couldn't help it; I flinched when he touched my bare shoulder.

"Why, Annie? Why were you scared? I was only being nice to you. I'd never do anything to hurt you." His expression—well, it drooped, his eyes and mouth turning down.

"I know."

"I just wanted to show you that I appreciate you," he said. The flat, casual tone of his words had the opposite effect that they probably intended.

I was petrified.

All my muscles tensed as he pulled the blanket down to my waist. I suspected that if I tugged it back up, it would anger him. Instinctively, I curled up on my side. My skin prickled all over, and my nipples reflexively pushed against the cool satin of the gown I was wearing. I crossed my arms over my front, folding in on myself like origami.

He yanked the blanket all the way down the bed, until it puddled on the floor at the end. I shivered.

"It does look nice on you." He smiled indulgently, like he was admiring a piece of art by a preschooler.

Preschooler. Stella! Jesus, Jake must be out of his mind right now, I realized. What was he thinking? Was he looking for me?

Where was my goddamn phone? I looked around the room, but didn't even see my clothes from earlier, much less my purse.

He cocked his head, stepping in front of me. "Are you looking for the rest? I can't wait to see the bra and panties on you."

No. *No.*

When he bent over to take some of the satin by my ankles between his fingers, my mouth went dry. "I nearly went with red, but I think the ivory suits you so much better. Pure." He frowned and stepped back. "But I don't know how pure you are, anymore."

Lying on my side, my line of sight was nearly level with the bulge clearly forming in his dress pants. My stomach churned.

I pushed myself up to a sitting position on the bed, folding my knees to my chest and wrapping my arms around myself. "Thank you for the gifts, John. They were very, um, thoughtful."

"You threw them away."

Well, no shit.

I bit my lip. "I'm sorry the flowers died," I said carefully. *Should have gotten me a potted plant, asshole.* "I still have all your beautiful notes. Did you pick out all those quotes yourself?"

"I love poetry," he said. "There's so much there that isn't said. Just like you and me."

I nodded. "Thank you." *What the hell was he talking about?*

He reached his hand out toward my face. I shifted my position before he could touch me.

"I need to call Evie," I told him. "She's picking me up after wo—" I stopped. What time was it?

He shook his head. "It's fine. I told her you went home early."

But I didn't! I didn't go home!

My chest tightened. If I were home right now, I wouldn't be *here*! My arms banded around my legs as words and ideas and pictures collided in my head.

Home was with Jake, in his arms. With Stella. Home wasn't here anymore. It wasn't a place; it was a person. A feeling. An after.

He would be looking for me. *They* would be looking for me. The sudden certainty of it brought a little relief.

I squirmed, realizing with dread that I was going to have to get off the bed. I was going to have to unfold myself and stand in front of John, shielded only by the thin gown and my fear.

"I have to go to the bathroom," I announced.

His eyes widened. "Oh." Maybe he hadn't considered that human need.

"May I?"

His gaze clung to me like the satin gown that I was trying to stop from riding up my thighs as I stretched my toes to the floor. He was still too close for comfort.

He watched me move in slow motion, watched me shiver. He'd watched me sleep.

"I really have to go," I said, hoping he'd give me more space.

He stepped back. "Of course."

My body relaxed a little, but when I stood up I felt dizzy. Cold.

I stumbled, pitching forward until his hand wrapped around my wrist like a manacle.

"I'll help you."

JAKE

*a*t first I was confused and irritated. Now I was panicking.

Actually, panic was not the right word for what I was feeling. It was more like a bone-bleaching, lightning strike of pure terror. The mixture of fury and guilt whipped the storm in my head up to paralyzing proportions.

Annie wasn't at home.

My apartment was dark and silent. Everything looked exactly the way it had earlier when I left to spend the rest of the afternoon and evening at the office—even the row of juice boxes on the coffee table.

By the time we backtracked to the restaurant, it had just closed. One of the remaining staff said something about an accident, and the manager taking Annie to the hospital.

"What kind of accident?" Dom asked. My heart roared in my ears.

The guy—a dishwasher—hadn't seen it happen, but rumor had it that there was lots of blood. Beyond implying that Annie's arm needed to be sewed back on, he couldn't give us much more.

At least we knew where she was, now. Probably. Hopefully. There were only half a dozen hospitals within a twenty-mile radius—unless she'd gone to some kind of urgent care clinic. *Shit.*

She still wasn't answering her phone, though, and the only result of my other calls was a dirty look from my brother when I chucked my phone at the dashboard.

"Goddamn hospitals won't tell me anything, not even if she showed up in the ER. Bullshit privacy laws."

"That's why people get married," Evie piped up from the back seat.

"What?"

The car swerved slightly as Dom and I both snapped our heads around to look at her. My phone slid across the dash and fell on my feet. I cursed as I reached down for it; Dom tightened his fingers on the steering wheel.

"Ignore me," she said. "I'm delirious from hunger. I'm about ready to gnaw on the headrest."

"Shit, baby, I'm sorry." My pussy-whipped brother pulled into a drive-through and proceeded to order more food than anyone should eat at eleven o'clock at night.

"No salt on the fries, but extra pickles on the burger," she reminded him.

Right. Evie was pregnant. "Maybe we should take you home," I thought out loud.

"We could go home and wait for her there," she suggested.

No way. I had every intention of driving to emergency rooms to physically see if Annie was there.

We dropped Evie off at my place in case Annie

came in, then Dom and I split up to hit the hospitals. It was late—very late—when we got back to find Evie asleep in my guest room.

"Just stay," I told my brother, rubbing my eyes. "No point in waking her up now." He was already stripping down to his boxer briefs and crawling into bed beside her. She sighed as he wrapped himself around her.

Watching Dom burrow his head into the honey-colored hair at the nape of Evie's neck made my throat hurt. For the first time in a long time, I physically ached in envy.

I *wanted* that—tonight, tomorrow night, every New Year's Eve.

Where the fuck was Annie?

Staring at my phone, I shuffled back into the living room and fell onto the couch. The knot in my chest that had been pulling tighter and tighter all night now felt as though it was going to rise up my throat and choke me.

A second wave of panic made my hands shake as I punched out a rapid text to Sheila. As soon as I pressed *Send*, I said, "Fuck it," and called instead.

"Jake? What is it?"

She sounded pretty awake for two in the morning.

"Is Stella okay?"

"Of course she is; she's fast asleep." *Yawn.*

"Can you just go check on her?" I winced, waiting for her to argue with me and complain.

The line was silent. Then I heard rustling noises, and Sheila sighed heavily into the phone. "Okay, I'll call you right back."

Time stretched out, thirty seconds feeling like thirty minutes. Even though I was waiting for it, I still jumped when the phone rang in my hand with an incoming video call.

"See?" Sheila whispered in the background as my screen filled with a dim image of Stella.

Only her head stuck out from under a blanket that looked like a star-filled night sky. A light shaped like a moon hung on the wall by her bed, casting enough of a glow for me to see the way she pouted in her sleep.

The knot in my chest loosened a fraction. "Okay. Thanks."

The image bobbed and blurred, and I heard a door shutting. Sheila turned the camera back on her own face. "Everything okay with you?"

I swallowed carefully. "Yeah. Just had a bad dream and wanted to see her. Sorry for waking you."

"She's fine, Jake. Fast asleep in her bed."

After apologizing again and ending the call, I went to my bedroom to think. As soon as I lay down Annie's scent wafted up from the sheets.

Fuck.

The smell of her shampoo was on the pillowcase. If I were to be honest—and an asshole—I'd admit that it was mixed with stale drool from her sleeping with her mouth open. If I were an honest asshole *in love*, I'd admit that the verdant, musky scent made me hard as I lay there.

Where was she?

My mind went to all sorts of horrible places. I'd seen a lot of shit over the years, and I didn't need a vivid imagination to think of some sickening situation that Annie could be in.

I jumped out of bed, trying to escape my own restlessness and worry. I walked around the apartment, thinking.

Stared at the door to the guest bedroom, remembering her first night there. Our first night.

"I don't fall in love."

She'd been in my bed every night since.

Down the hall, I stood in the doorway of Stella's room. At least she was safe in her own bed, if not this one.

Holy shit.

I pivoted so quickly that I stumbled and bounced off the wall. How could I have not thought of it?

Her own bed.

Her own bed.

JAKE

*A*nnie still wasn't answering her phone. Something had to be wrong.

I didn't know where her fob and apartment key were. And for all that I'd reminded her that her stalker could get into her building, I was having a damn hard time of it. There weren't as many people going in and out at dark o'clock to make it easy to slip through the doors.

I bounced on my toes by the front steps, considering what to do next. Fuck! I hated this.

If I started ringing buzzers of random apartments, there was a chance that someone would let me in. There was also a chance that someone could call the police—which might not be the worst thing. When they showed up, I might be able to convince them to go upstairs and check the apartment.

I was on the verge of doing just that when a cab pulled up in front of the building and a drunken, amorous couple got out. They stumbled toward the concrete steps, holding on to each other as they climbed to the door.

Thank god for a late last call. Thank god for one night stands. Thank god they were too into each other to notice me, or how I shoved my foot in the door to stop it from closing after them.

I didn't bother waiting for the elevator, instead taking the stairs two at a time. When I got to her floor, though, I hesitated. It was so damn quiet. If I banged on the door, I'd run the risk of waking the neighbors.

Then again, for all I knew it was one of the neighbors that was stalking her.

I put my ear to the door, deciding that if I heard something, I'd start knocking.

Whump!

I jerked my head back as I heard a grunt.

A wordless cry.

My heart stopped, then restarted at double-time.

"Annie!" I slammed my fist against the door, adrenaline and fear surging through my body. *"Annie!"* My hand tugged at the door knob.

Godfuckingdammit! Of course, the door was locked. A crash came from inside.

I started thumping. Kicking. Ramming with my shoulder. The door creaked, but it wasn't as easy to bust down as movies made it look.

A door down the hall opened; a head popped out before disappearing again. Breathing hard and my body and brain reverting back to the sandbox, I jumped back and lifted my leg in a powerful front kick.

Slam! Slam! Slam!

"Jaaa—!" I heard her voice inside.

My frustration burst from my body in a growl and stronger kicks.

Wham! Wham! Wham!

Another door—the wrong one—opened, and a middle-aged man stepped into the hallway.

"Hey!"

Wham! "Someone's got my girlfriend in there!"

He strode down the hall, and when I glanced over he had a *"Shit, do I want to get involved?"* expression on his face—and a golf club.

I seized the club out of his hand and started whacking away at the doorknob.

"What the he—!"

The shaft vibrated in my hands at the metal on metal contact.

"Hey! You're gonna pay for that!"

I looked down at the glorified tuning fork with disgust. It wasn't much better than a miniature golf putter. I let out a roar of frustration and gave it all I had —and gouged the doorframe. The man jumped out of the way as I tossed the club aside.

"Jake!"

He stepped toward the door. "Is that her? Did you call the police?"

I backed up to the opposite wall. "Either help or get the fuck out of my way." I took two powerful strides and raised my leg again.

Wham!

The frame around the door splintered.

Finally.

I was about to lose my mind, not knowing what was happening inside. I took another run at the door, but this time Golf Club Guy put his shoulder into it as well.

Whump!

Two more kicks together and the door bust open.

When I got inside, I found Annie swinging around on the back of a man like a cape, her arm around his neck.

My ninja girl.

Her white dress was bunched up to her waist as she tried to wrap her legs around the guy, her creamy bare ass hanging out.

If the previous few minutes had been the longest of my life, then time flashed by in a split second as I stomped my foot into the back of the guy's knee. As he went down, I caught Annie by the waist and pulled her off him.

She fell against me, trembling and close to hyperventilating. Her skin was chilled, but her face was red.

I needed to hold her; to make sure she was okay. The fact that she clearly wasn't wearing underwear was freaking me out. What the fuck had happened?

But more importantly, I needed to beat the shit out of… her boss?

Annie clung to my arm as I kicked the back of his other knee as he moved to get up. Golf Club Guy elbowed us aside and sat down on the fucker's thighs as he face planted on the wooden floor.

"I called the police," he said, huffing a little as he straddled John and held the club to the back of his neck.

I nodded, sweeping Annie into my arms. She'd never seemed so slight, so tiny as she was right at that moment. I knew she was tough, but the memory of her frightened voice reverberated in my brain. I started to carry her over to the bed, but she yelped and dug her fingers into me.

"No! Not there!"

I wanted to puke. What. The. Fuck. Happened?

Cradling her to me like I would Stella, I carried her into the bathroom. Fell back against the door, slamming it shut. Slid to the floor, my legs stretched out, Annie in my lap.

My head banged against the door. Our chests rose and fell together, as though our hearts beat harder as one.

"Annie, honey…"

The silky gown she wore was slippery under my fingers, and I longed to feel the warmth of her skin. Her whole body stiffened as I ran my hands over her—a marble statue—then she crumpled into gulping sobs.

"I'm not… hurt…" she managed to get out.

I didn't believe her. "It's okay." I buried my face in her hair as she shook against me.

The sound of a siren grew louder, whooping to a finish nearby.

She sucked in a breath, but it didn't seem to fill her lungs. "I'm sorry." Sniffled.

"It's okay." There was nothing to be sorry for, unless she was sorry that she—or I—didn't get to kill the motherfucker. I bit back a demand to know where her phone was, and sighed.

Reaching out with one arm, I awkwardly tugged a towel off the bar by the bathtub. Her shudders began to subside as I wrapped it around her. Noises penetrated the door behind us, voices in the living room.

We held on to each other.

ANNIE

"*I* don't want to go back to work."

"No shit." Jake snorted as we lay in bed.

I luxuriated in his arms, feeling no desire to move. *I could live here forever.*

It had been three weeks since… since.

It took most of the first two days to finish with the police and assure everyone that I hadn't been raped. My security had been assaulted, and my self-assurance molested, but John hadn't really touched me. Or hurt me.

Just scared the shit out of me.

Jake and the EMTs had made me go to the hospital, but other than some GHB in my system and a sore body and soul there wasn't anything wrong with me.

For the next few days I curled up on the couch in my sweats, under a blanket—at times too hot, but I preferred it to the alternative.

My nerves were frazzled for the first week. My whole body was sore from the effort of trying *not* to cry when I saw Stella. For someone who didn't like crying, though, it had become my new hobby.

I cried when Evie came over.

I cried in the shower.

I cried when Dominic handed me a bottle of water to rehydrate. *Jerk*.

Now, I was all cried out. And much calmer. I'd begun seeing a therapist, at Evie's insistence, but I really felt better. It was like I got it out of my system, and then closed the door on it. Jake said something about post-traumatic stress, which I waved off.

I was—*would be*—fine. I was a survivor. I had a force field of people around me, a restraining order, and an online wish-list full of self-help books that I would never get around to reading.

John had been charged with assault and unlawful confinement, among a few other things. And he'd been fired. The restaurant's owners put me on paid sick leave —without tips, of course—but I had given them no return date.

"You don't have to go back to work, honey," Jake reminded me, his nose rubbing against my neck.

I hummed. Part of me felt like I should; get back up on that horse and all that stuff—but the rest of me felt like I'd found a new calling in life, just lying in Jake's arms.

I'd earned a break, and for the first time I had the breathing room to figure out what I wanted to do next.

I frowned. "You know that if I don't go back to the restaurant then Evie's going to put me to work with wedding planning."

The date had been moved up—a lot—to accommo-date Evie's pregnancy. I wondered out loud to her what kind of honeymoon they would have if she was too far along to have sex. When she told me all the different ways it was possible, I was sorry I mentioned it at all.

"That reminds me, you still haven't confirmed as my 'plus one.'"

I shifted, straddling my boyfriend. His hands went my hips, toying with the elastic of my panties, and a smile stretched over his face.

He could have been smiling at me, or at the "Self-Rescuing Princess" t-shirt I wore to bed.

Either way, I loved making him smile.

"I'm not fucking you in the coat room. I told you that."

"Well, shit." He ran his hands up and down my sides, curving around from the bottom of my shoulder blades to the swell of my ass. "There are no other bridesmaids. What am I supposed to do now?"

"Besides," I said, squirming on top of him, "Stella agreed to be my date."

"Stella is the flower girl. She has to be there, anyhow."

"So do you!" I pushed down on the hard muscles of his chest.

"So we'll go as a family."

I froze. "What?"

"You. Me. Stella. All dressed up, with someplace to go."

"Oh."

His eyes narrowed. "No?"

Yes. *Yes!*

I bit my lip. "I, uh, just didn't think that was the kind of threesome you were into."

"Ewwwww!" His face twisted as his fingers tickled up

my sides. I giggled, relaxing in relief that he didn't take my joke the wrong way. That little episode with Evie—both of ours—had been forgiven and forgotten. We'd moved on.

He made a horrified, retching sound. Tickled me again.

"Okay, I'm sorry! I didn't mean it!" I swayed on top of him, breathless with giggles. Laughter was an amazing antidote to just about anything in life. I'd learned that once I'd stopped crying.

"Ugh!" he spat out, but his eyes creased at the sides with a mischievous grin. "That's our daughter you're talking about!"

Our daughter? I lost my balance in surprise, my forearms falling to his chest. It was a slip of the tongue; that was all. Our bodies moved together as we breathed, ebbing up and down like a boat on a lake.

"We'll go as a family," he repeated.

His expression was serious, and there was a glint in his eye that looked like challenge. Or pride. Or both.

I shrugged. "Weird family. The billionaire, single dad, toy store tycoon—"

"Not single anymore," he interrupted. "Okay, the billionaire—" He paused to roll his eyes. "—toy tycoon and the ball-busting ninja waitress. And their trusty sidekick."

"Not a waitress anymore," I amended, wrinkling my nose at him. "And you know we can't trust our sidekick."

We'd been working on keeping Stella out of our bed. She had a tendency to turn sideways as she slept, like a human clock face, her legs flailing all night long. Recently she'd wanted to snuggle between us, and we moved her back to her bed after she fell asleep—mostly.

The times that we didn't were an exercise in fatigue management the next day.

"It sounds like a comic book," I said.

He nodded. When I went to push myself up, he pulled me back down. Stared at me. "I love you, Annie. You know that, right?"

He'd never said the words before—not out loud, not on purpose.

"I love you. I—" I stopped.

I felt like I should say more.

There was so much more in my heart and soul, but there weren't words for it all. I'd need a dictionary, a thesaurus, and many, many years to express it all. I sighed, meeting his foolish, abashed grin with one of my own.

Leaning forward, I kissed him. Softly, then harder. Open mouth, touching my tongue to his. Tasting him. Inviting him into me.

His hips tilted, pressing his growing arousal into me. I wriggled in response, making him moan. This was my new favorite position when fooling around, and he had no complaints.

I rocked against him, my core dampening. Softening. Tingling. Needing him. Reflexively, his fingers tightened over my hips and pulled me down to grind into him. The expression on his face flattened out in apology; his hands fell to the bed.

We hadn't had sex—like, *sex* sex—since… *since*, but only because he didn't want to push me.

I decided to push him.

I circled my hips, pushing down on him.

"Annie…"

"Jake…" I mocked his serious tone. "You don't like it when I beg, remember?"

He didn't make me beg—or wait. With swift fingers, he pulled away all the barriers between us, and sunk into me with a groan.

"Oh my god, yes!" My eyes fluttered shut at the feeling of pure completion. I couldn't keep them closed though; I needed to look at him. Needed to be connected to him in every way I could.

His jaw flexed as we began moving together. "Fuck, Annie. I missed you."

"I missed you, too. Missed this," I panted. He drove up into me, filling all the nooks and crannies of loneliness left inside me. This was going to be a short-lived coming-together, but we had time.

Lots of time.

Our hands wove together on his chest, curling into shared fists as we pulled each other up to the top of our climax. It was clichéd to shout our love for each other as we came, but that didn't make it any less true.

The scary part was over.

This was the blissful part.

This was the *after*.

Now it's The End, or the final Happy Ever After!

~

I hope you enjoyed these stories! I loved writing all these characters, but I confess that Jake and Annie are my favorite.

Check the *About the Author* section for my social

media links so you can stay up to date. Or you can join my mailing list by going to http://www.nikkykaye.com to sign up.

Thanks again for reading!
Nikky

ALSO BY NIKKY KAYE

A Billion Reasons

A Model Fiancé

A Slip of the Tongue

A Screw Loose

THE BILLIONAIRE BOOK CLUB

The Billionaire's Makeover

The Billionaire's Roommate

The Billionaire's Homecoming

The Billionaire's Mafia Bride

The Billionaire's Secret Baby

ACKNOWLEDGMENTS

My thanks to Gavin Grace and Nick Keller for the amazing cover photo and Sarah Hansen of Okay Creations for making it out of this world.

Give Me Books helped me get out the word in their own patient, inimitable, patient, professional fashion. I also have to thank Jessica Estep and Inkslinger PR for their last minute dive-bombing (and the beginning of our partnership).

I have a ton of help in my professional and personal lives. Notable among the superheroes around me are: Amanda Walker, Vivian Tabonda, Crystal Kook, Angela Evans, Kristen Echo, and (as always) Dr. Kaye.

Lastly, I want to thank my loyal fans, and ever expanding readership and author tribe. Every day I get to interact with readers who make me laugh and authors who make me go all fan-girly. I'm so lucky!

This is a tough business. We live in our heads, on our computers, and online. Sometimes it feels strangely artificial, until I remember the real emotions evoked when I'm engrossed in a good book. I can't wait to read the next one on my TBR and to write the next story in my head.

This book is the result of a goofy challenge between myself and superstar author Maya Hughes in the summer of 2017.

To be perfectly honest, I began this book as a joke, sort of over-the-top satire. I wanted to see what would happen if I threw everything I could into a super sexy, sassy book. In fact, the working title was "Tropa-palooza." Turns out, it was a hell of a lot of fun!

Thanks for reading!

N

ABOUT THE AUTHOR

I love reading and writing funny, sexy stories. I am over-educated and under-organized, and have a terrible habit of adding more books to my Kindle than I can possibly read.

My only experience with auctions is eBay and I've never had a threesome or a stalker. Or maybe I have, and I'm just not telling you! But today, the biggest risk I took was having cotton candy for dinner. And it was delicious.

Want the scoop on new books and contests! Join my Coming Attractions newsletter at http://subscribepage.com/nikkykaye

You can find me hiding in my car with my laptop, or at:
www.nikkykaye.com
read@nikkykaye.com

f facebook.com/officialnikkykayebooks

instagram.com/nikkykayebooks

BB bookbub.com/authors/nikky-kaye

twitter.com/readnikkykaye